THE TENDER DECEPTION

When Sophia Barton was taken from Curton Workhouse to be a scullery-maid at Perriman Court, her future looked bleak. Was it really an act of Providence that persuaded Lady Perriman to adopt her as her ward? Sophia was brought up together with the Perriman children, and before sailing with his regiment for India, George, the heir to the title, declared his love. But tragedy hit the family and Sophia found herself caught up in a web of mystery and intrigue.

LAURA ROSE

THE TENDER DECEPTION

Complete and Unabridged

LINFORD
Leicester

First published in Great Britain in 1975 by
Robert Hale and Company
London

First Linford Edition
published 1999
by arrangement with
Robert Hale Limited
London

British Library CIP Data

Rose, Laura
    The tender deception.—Large print ed.—
Linford romance library
    1. Love stories
    2. Large type books
    I. Title
    823.9'14 [F]

    ISBN 0–7089–5489–8

Published by
F. A. Thorpe (Publishing) Ltd.
Anstey, Leicestershire

Set by Words & Graphics Ltd.
Anstey, Leicestershire
Printed and bound in Great Britain by
T. J. International Ltd., Padstow, Cornwall

This book is printed on acid-free paper

Prologue

'Stand still, you lousy little bastard unless you want me to cut your lug off.'

The harsh words didn't make me flinch, partly because they were true and partly because I was so accustomed to hearing them, but to stand still, was an impossibility.

The damp brick floor of the wash-house, sent shivers up through my naked body, but listening to Mrs. Mathews and Mrs. Needler who was cutting off my louse infested hair, caused me to tremble still more violently. What was going to happen to me? Where would I be sent? Who would be my mistress?

Mrs. Needler stood back to survey her handiwork and then decided she could make a still closer crop, at the same time asking, 'Why is the Board meeting earlier than usual?'

Mrs. Mathews picked up a lock of my hair and took a long look at it. 'Doesn't it curl nicely? Wish my Debbie's would curl like this.' Then she dropped it quickly and struck her hands together, as though they had been contaminated.

'Why are we meeting early? Well, along comes this fine lady and says she wants a girl for her kitchen. 'Very good, ma'am,' I says. 'We have several girls ready to go out. The Board meets three o'clock, Monday.' Then, 'Dear, oh dear', says my lady. 'I have to return to Yorkshire that day.'

'Yorkshire?'

'Yes. Yorkshire. So I up and says, 'Have you no foundlings in Yorkshire then?' And she smiles in her ladylike way and says, 'Oh yes, but there are reasons why I prefer a girl from Lancashire.' '

'Did she give her reasons? Are they better workers, or do they eat less?'

'She didn't say because she went

on about the long journey and how she wanted to be on her way, so I asked Mr. Mathews and he arranged this early meeting. What's more, her Ladyship says, 'About the apprentice fee. Pray keep it to buy extras for the children,' ' and at that Mrs. Mathews went into a roar of laughter, causing her double chin to wobble in a most fascinating way. 'Five guineas, Mrs. Needler! Just think of the gin that'll buy.'

Mrs. Needler was now soaping her hands in the large rain barrel from which steam was rising and the next moment was lathering my shorn head. Some of the soap ran into my eyes and stung painfully, but I dare not cry out. Then, without any warning I was lifted and dropped into the barrel of water. For a moment I was panic stricken. They were going to drown me! Then as the warm water seeped through my flesh I was aware of a new pleasure . . . an intoxicating, languorous pleasure, for it was my very first hot bath in all my nine years. Mrs. Needler was now cupping water over my head and I was loving every moment of it, when suddenly with one hand, she seized me by the nose, and with the other pushed my head under water. Now I was sure I was going to drown. I had seen death from drowning in the canal that ran down by the side of the workhouse, here at Curton.

I don't know whether I struggled or shouted, but then, miracle of miracles, my head was above water again and my tormentors rocking with laughter.

'Here,' said Mrs. Needler, handing me the piece of rough soap, 'wash your legs and arms, otherwise her Ladyship might turn up her aristocratic nose, should you go near her.'

I don't want to go near her, I thought. I don't want to go to a strange place like Yorkshire, away from the people I know, but I'd heard Mrs. Mathews saying it was time I was placed . . . nine years old . . . I should have been placed two years ago!

I wanted again to feel the hot water seeping through my body, so as the women went on with their talking, I daringly knelt down and swished it over my shoulders. I had never felt so light-hearted in all my life, but the pleasure was short-lived, for I was unceremoniously dragged from the barrel, stood on the floor and given a stinging slap across the buttocks.

'Did you see what she was doing? Goes to show the badness in her. Just what we were talking about the other day . . . about the loose living of these society folk . . . bathing every day; no wonder there's so much wickedness about . . . '

'That's nothing to what I heard only yesterday.' Mrs. Mathews must have beckoned to Mrs. Needler, because she stopped rubbing me down and stepped away, but not far enough to prevent me hearing their conversation, even though it was carried on in a whisper.

'That Queen of France . . . who had her head chopped off . . . what did they call her? Oh I remember — Marie Antoinette. Well, they do say,' her voice went still lower, 'they do say she wore some kind of men's trousers under her petticoats . . . can you think of anything more disgusting?'

Mrs. Needler made an exclamation of horror. 'No wonder she got her head chopped off. She deserved it.'

She handed me an unbleached calico shift. 'Put that on. Now the frock.'

It was a grey stuff dress, but absolutely new. The first new garment I had ever worn. There was also a pair of shoes, cheap and clumsy, but never-the-less brand new.

'Now go and sit in the Board room and don't speak to anyone . . . and don't dare soil that frock.'

I did as I was told, and took a seat to await the other girls who were to come before the committee.

'Please God,' I prayed, 'Don't let the Yorkshire lady choose me.' The thought of strange people and strange places terrified me. I'd heard about mistresses who beat their apprentices, not that we didn't get our fair share here.

I looked down at my clean feet and legs, and wondered when they would get their next wash. Would there be a canal, where I could paddle and then I remembered that I was going out to work, not to play. The canal had been a favourite playground of mine. On a summer day you could sit on the side and dangle your feet, or walk along the shallow water, trying to scoop up the little black minnows, but there were times, after the rain or snow, when it flooded its' banks and it was dangerous to go near. More than one foundling had been drowned and we were threatened with beatings if we were found playing near by.

The most exciting happening that I could remember was when a man was dragged out, believed to be drowned. Two or three of the standers-by sat on him, punched him and kneeded him, all trying to bring him back to life.

Then another man knelt down beside him, took his face in both his hands and breathed into his mouth. He did this over and over again. Then the man actually came back to life! After that, it was our favourite game. Some of us would pretend to be drowned and the others would kneel down and breath into our mouths until we jumped up, brought back to life! It was a lovely, exciting game until someone saw us and told Mrs. Mathews. Then we were whipped more severely than I could remember and the parson came and gave us a sermon on the sins of the flesh and all its' wickedness.

The other girls had now joined me and then the parish council trooped in, headed by the beadle, Mr. Mathews, with Mrs. Mathews bringing up the rear. My lungs seemed to be swelling to bursting point as along with the others, I stood up and bobbed a curtsey. After a few minutes conversation between themselves, Mrs. Mathews opened the door and called, 'Lady Perriman.'

As the newcomer entered, I looked at her with fear in my heart. She was a tall lady and wore a cloak of russet coloured wool topped by a big fur collar. She wore no hat or hood, and I saw that her long ringlets were tinged with grey, and her face, though serious, had a gentle, soft look. Another woman, who had followed her into the room, thin, sparse, and dressed entirely in black, kept in the background.

I was roused from my scrutiny by Mr. Mathews bellowing loudly, 'Ill-mannered sluts . . .'

He had no need to continue, for hurriedly, we all three rose to our feet and bobbed another curtsey.

Then I heard my name called and falteringly, I stepped forward. A clerk droned out my short lived history. Sophia Barton. Aged nine. Born 1790. Parentage unknown. Took my name from foster parents, but foster mother died of the pox seven years ago, since which time I had been in the foundlings home. Health good. Behaviour good.

As her ladyship could see, clean, well-dressed, well-fed. After the other girls had had their records read out, Lady Perriman gave us each a long, intent scrutiny, and then asked, 'Who do you think, Martha?'

Now it was Martha who came and stared keenly, as though looking for flaws, and then, turning her back on us whispered to her mistress.

What I had feared now came about, because it was my name that I heard pass between her ladyship and Mr. Mathews. I wanted to cry out in protest, for the unknown held terror for me, but I spoke not a word; it was more than I dare do.

Martha now took me by the arm to stand by her side while the articles were drawn up and signed, binding me in Lady Perriman's service until I was twenty-one.

Twenty-one! I should be an old woman by then ... if I lived to that age. The parson, who came each Sunday to the Institution, never tired of threatening us with the terrible fate of nine-year-old Mary Wotton who ran away from her mistress, stealing some money, and was publicly hung for her wickedness. Every now and then a boy or girl would run away from the workhouse, but they were nearly always caught, brought back and whipped, and then manacled to a wall, their only food being dry bread and water. Never-the-less, I had already made up my mind to run away from Yorkshire.

Now her Ladyship was speaking. 'My carriage is outside so we can be on our way. What about the girl's belongings? Are they packed?'

'Packed?' Mrs. Mathews looked astounded. 'She has nothing to pack, ma'am . . . As you can see, we have rigged her out with new clothes. Perhaps we could find some sort of a bonnet to cover up that . . . ' She gave a sniggering laugh indicating my shorn head, only to be interupted by, 'No need to bother. I have a cloak and hood in the carriage. What I meant, were there any personal belongings?'

Mrs. Mathews shook her head vigorously. 'None at all, ma'am. None.'

'Then I will bid you all good day.' She inclined her head to the committee, who in return rose from their chairs and bowed low, Mrs. Mathews finalising our departure with a quick bob.

I walked out to the waiting carriage, inwardly trembling, but now a new sensation was the cause . . . not fear . . . but excitement.

★ ★ ★

I had never before been in a carriage. Martha reached in and brought out a cloak, which curiously enough was just about my size, pulling the hood well over my head. Then with her Ladyship seated, she pushed me in, herself following, and the footman closing the door.

I felt so strange that I was too shy to look about me, keeping my eyes on the fur rug, sensing the comfort of the seat and the sweet pungent smell of the leather.

'When did you last eat child?' It was Lady Perriman speaking, I still dare not look at her, but managed to mumble that it had been at six o'clock that morning.

From under the coach seat, Martha dragged out a flat basket and placed it beside her on the seat. Curiosity made me look up as she opened it, and then immediately, I realised how hungry I was; how dry was my throat. There, neatly packed, were pasties and cakes such as I had never seen before and I needed no encouragement to help myself, taking a pasty in each hand and eating greedily, my hunger overcoming my shyness.

There followed milk to quench my thirst and more pasties and sweet cake until Martha stopped me with her sharp spoken 'no more' followed by Lady Perriman's almost whispered, 'Later on . . . you can eat again.'

How long I slept, I do not know, for when I awakened it was to the sound of hooves and wheels on a cobbled courtyard; to the 'Whoas' of the coachman; the shouting of orders to stable boys and the comings and goings of the tavern servants, where we were staying for the night.

It was dark and lanterns were being held high as we were assisted to alight. Now my fears were returning. Where was I being taken?

Martha was making the necessary arrangements with the tavern keeper and within minutes we were following a maid.

Flinging open the door, she said tartly, 'There. The best bedroom in the house for my lady,' and then opening the next door, and addressing Martha, 'You and the little Miss in here.'

Martha pushed me in and put down the candle the maid had handed her. 'Get undressed and into bed . . . I must see to my Lady,' and going out of the room, closed the door. There was only the candle and its flickering, dancing flame increased the eeriness of the room. Should I run away now, while I had the chance? True, they had fed me and treated me kindly, but perhaps that was their cunning way of calming my fears.

I opened the door cautiously. There was no one about. I tip-toed outside. There was a faint feeble light, coming from Lady Perriman's room, which meant the door must be slightly ajar. Could I get by without being noticed?

I went as far as the door, and then hesitated. I could hear Lady Perriman's soft voice, but couldn't make out what what she was saying. My low, vulgar upbringing urged me to listen. I stepped still nearer, my ear to the opening. It was easy to hear Martha.

'There. There, my lady. You've done the right thing, so now stop all your wittering. When we get home tomorrow, you'll find everything will work out all right.'

'But just how, I don't know

Martha . . . ' Her voice trailed away, so that I couldn't hear until . . . 'Go and see if she's in bed. Get her some hot milk . . . She needs building up, poor little lamb . . . '

Little lamb? That was the first time I had been called a pet name. Fearing that Martha would catch me eavesdropping, I went quickly back to the room next door and was about to get into bed when she came in.

'My. That's taken you a long time. Here, drink this milk and then to sleep. We shall be away early in the morning.' Wearing only the calico shift, I crouched down between the sheets and was greatly relieved when Martha went out of the room again. The idea of sleeping with an adult person frightened me, but the warm milk combined with the darkness soon over-rode my fears and I slept soundly until morning.

★ ★ ★

I started the day badly, grumbling when Martha poured water into the wash-basin and told me to wash. In vain, I protested that I'd been washed yesterday, only to get a sharp retort ' . . . and from now on, you'll wash every day, or else . . . ' but when she saw how badly I had been flea-bitten during the night, she was all concern. The bites had irritated; I had scratched, and now my skin was red and angry.

'I'll get you some ointment when you have washed.' She shrugged her shoulders. 'They no longer bite me. I'm too tough. Still it's no use complaining. Even the King has to keep a resident flea-catcher.'

She gave me soap and face flannel and, standing over me, saw to it that I washed my neck and ears. Then as I found the soap so fragrantly scented. I lingered over the process. and there she was, scolding that I should hurry.

The liniment stung, but as the serving maid now brought in my breakfast, I forgot about the fleas and greedily set about eating. There was cold meat and bread and a mug of milk. I ate every morsel. What Lady Perriman and Martha had for breakfast I do not know, for within what seemed a very short time we were back in the carriage and on our last stage home.

Perhaps, I argued with myself, my future might not be too bad. It depended what they were going to do with me. I had already decided that sooner or later I would run away but in the meantime, I might as well eat all that came my way.

* * *

The countryside was not becoming less rugged; jagged, scarred hill-sides becoming more softly undulating; lush green meadows taking the place of scrubby gorse-covered moors.

Throughout the journey, I frequently dozed, and it wasn't until I noticed that we were driving along a straight roadway, on either side of which were rows of trees, all growing in the most orderly manner, that I began to look about me with curiosity. The regimented trees now gave way to open parkland, and then we stopped abruptly as we came to a wrought-iron gateway, barring the road. On either side were two small cottages, both with pretty flower-filled gardens; From out of one, as though expecting us, a woman came, and quickly opened the gates, bobbing a curtsey as we passed through. Now we were driving through grassy woodland, with the branches of old, gnarled trees forming a canopy, but when we startled a deer, browsing near the roadway, I gave a cry of alarm. I had never before seen such a monstrous, horned creature, but Lady Perriman put a soothing hand over mine. 'Soon be home. When we turn into the avenue, we shall see the house.'

Then we were passing the stables; horses were being exercised round the cobbled courtyard, while others were being rubbed down and groomed. What

19

in the world did they do with all these horses? More boys were cleaning harnesses, others polishing coach work, but all stopped to raise their caps as our coach rolled on to the front of the house.

How can I describe *Perriman Court*? No King's palace, I was sure, could be so big or so beautiful. No king could have such beautiful smooth lawns; such beds of roses; such wonderful fountains, sending spray so high in the air.

Within an instant of stopping, footmen were there to let down the step, and to assist Lady Perriman to alight, with Martha and me following, and even as the ignorant child I was, the size and grandeur of the house and grounds moved me in a way I could not understand.

Lady Perriman was looking over the garden, down beyond the vast lawns, to what seemed like shimmering water.

She spoke quickly to Martha. 'What is happening down by the lake? All those people?' and as she spoke, we saw a man bend down and lift from the water, what appeared to be the body of a child.

'It's one of the children. I know it is,' she gasped, and regardless of everyone, picked up her voluminous skirts and ran towards the group by the lake side,

I looked at Martha. She couldn't run, but the coachman and the footmen were already following Lady Perriman. Why shouldn't I join in and see what was going on, and heedless of Martha, I too ran and soon overtook them all.

When I reached the lake side, they had put down the small, wet, bedraggled body, and a man was kneeding its chest and stomach.

'My God! Oh my God! It's George.' Lady Perriman's anguished shriek split the air, bringing the hub-hub of consternation and panic to a stunned silence.

She was down on her knees, attempting to cradle the boy's head while the man continued to pummel the inert body. 'It's Mama. Speak to me, George. Speak to Mama!'

From the crowd I heard a muttered voice. 'It's no use. He's a gonner.'

I don't know how I mustered the courage. Perhaps it was my workhouse impudence, but there I was kneeling down by the boy's supine body. I was remembering seeing the man brought back to life by the canal side . . . remembering the game we used to play.

Taking a deep breath, I put my mouth to the boy's and then breathed into it. Someone took hold of my shoulders, and would have dragged me off but I heard Lady Perriman's voice, no longer gentle and soft, but hard and quivering, 'Leave her alone. Leave her alone.'

I took another deep breath . . . and another almost to bursting point, before breathing into that wet, sagging, open mouth.

Then I heard several voices; a rustling murmur. 'He moved . . . Did you see?

Go on little lass . . . go on!'

I went on, and there beside me on the grass was Lady Perriman, cradling the boy in her arms, 'George, my darling. It's Mama. You're safe now George. Open your eyes and look at Mama!'

I watched the boy look up at his mother and saw the love between them as she kissed him again and again.

'Don't be angry . . . Mama . . . not with anyone else. It was my fault . . . I was looking for fish . . . '

At the sound of the barely audible voice, the tears streamed down her Ladyship's face, as she rocked the boy in her arms.

A footman stepped forward. 'Shall I take Master George Your Ladyship? Mutely she watched as the man lifted her wet, bedraggled son, while another assisted her to her feet, leaving me to follow.

It was then that I felt drained of all strength; I could have stayed there and gone to sleep. Her Ladyship, however, turned, and seeing me on the grass, still gasping for breath, called sharply to another lackey, 'Bruton . . . pick up Miss Sophia and carry her to the house and hand her over to Martha,' turning to me with a wan smile, 'We must both get out of our wet, dirty clothes, must we not Sophia?'

Miss Sophia! Carried by a liveried footman! Would wonders never cease?

I was hardly given time to notice the beautiful entrance hall or the thick, deep carpets for I was hurried upstairs into what I found to be the nursery and before I was aware of what was going on, there I was in a bath of hot water, with two nursery maids washing me.

My uppermost feeling was one of mortification, that these two maids, with whom I should most likely be working, should see my flea-bitten skin and my rough, coarse clothing and my shorn head.

Then the miracle happened. They were dressing me in pretty clothing . . . a soft, lace-edged shift, a petticoat with a deep frill of lace and then, most beautiful of all, a pink, flower-sprigged, muslin frock along with red kid shoes and long, white stockings. if only my head hadn't been shorn . . . but even that had been thought of, for there was a little white, lace cap to hide my lack of hair.

Without any comment or questions, one of the maids took me by the hand, down to Lady Perriman's room and in answer to her knock, I was pushed inside and the door closed behind me.

I had never before been in a bedroom. At the workhouse we had slept on straw palliasses on the floor of one big room devoid of all other furniture.

I looked at the canopied bed, with its blue silk hangings and the blue and white cover. There were several comfortable chairs and sofas, and beneath my feet, a thick carpet. Innumerable pictures and portraits adorned the walls and there were silver candlesticks on tables either side of the bed. The whole room was fragrant with some sweet perfume and as I stared about me in awe and wonderment, Lady Perriman, resting on a sofa, spoke gently.

'Come here, Sophia.' She took me by both hands and appraised me. 'Doesn't she look sweet, Martha?'

Martha tightened her mouth and raised her eyebrows. 'Don't turn the child's head, my lady,' but as she passed me on the way to hang a dress in the wardrobe, she patted my cheek, with, 'Yes. She looks very sweet.'

Now Lady Perriman had her arm around me. 'Sophia. You did a very wonderful thing today . . . you gave me back my son. If it hadn't been for you . . . ' Her voice choked . . . 'It seems as though God meant me to bring you here, this very day . . . so . . . Can you understand me, Sophia?'

I couldn't really, but I nodded mutely, ' . . . and because of that, I am going to bring you up as my ward. You shall be educated along with my children . . . will you like that Sophia?'

Again I nodded, although I had never wanted to learn to read and write. I saw no use for it.

'Then we will begin tomorrow. I shall tell the children and servants, that you are the child of a dear friend of mine. Just one thing, Sophia. Don't talk about the workhouse. I want you to forget all about it, and I don't want anyone asking you questions. Is that understood, Sophia?'

Again I could only nod, I was so overwhelmed by all that had happened and was going to happen.

'I want more than a nod, Sophia. I want your solemn promise. Say it after me. 'I promise I will never, never talk about the workhouse and to say that my mother is a friend of Lady Perriman's.

I repeated the words. Then Her Ladyship kissed me.

'You and George will be great

friends, and I shall never forget the debt I owe you. All I want to do now is to make you happy, and to give you a good upbringing.' She released me. 'Now back you go to the nursery. You'll soon overcome your shyness amongst the others.' I could feel her watching me, as I went out of the room, so at the door I turned and dropped her an awkward little bob of a curtsey and was rewarded with, 'Thank you darling. Thank you. You'll soon learn, I can plainly see.'

Outside the room I stood and stared around me. My heart was pounding furiously. Last night I had been a 'poor little lamb.' Now she was calling me 'darling'. It was all so unreal; as was this thickly carpeted corridor, with carpeted stairs leading both up and down. Which way should I go? Dare I open one of those doors?

As though in answer to my unspoken question, a girl came slowly down the stairs from the floor above. Although she was as tall as I was, she was obviously much younger, yet full of jaunty confidence.

'I'm Mary. You are to have tea with us in the nursery . . . but not George . . . he's still being sick, so . . . ' Her voice trailed away, but only for a moment, for she went on gleefully, 'We're having whim-wham Trifle. I love it. Do you?'

How could I plead my ignorance, but without waiting for an answer, the excited chatter went on, 'It was all my fault really. I dared George to wade out and grab a fish. Papa says a Perriman should never show fear . . . '

'Papa also says that a Perriman must never disobey.'

From behind us Martha's hard, angry voice cut into Mary's discourse. 'You have been forbidden to play by the lake-side, so . . . for your disobedience . . . no whim-wham for you . . . '

Such was my introduction to the Perriman household . . . the beginning of a happy orderly childhood; my transition from degredation to gracious living.

1

I awoke early that morning, not altogether happy, for overriding all the forthcoming excitement, I couldn't rid myself of a feeling of loss and desolation.

Tonight, Lady Perriman, or Aunt Lucy as I now called her, was holding a grand assembly for all the neighbouring gentry to wine and dine and dance, the occasion being George's leave-taking, prior to sailing to India with his regiment.

I knew that Aunt Lucy shared my sorrow as we had done from the first day he had gone away to school but then there was always the day to live for . . . the day when he came home for holidays. There would be no return from India for several years. Although I was his senior by fourteen months, I did not feel the difference,

31

chiefly because when I first entered the Perriman schoolroom, I could neither read nor write and it was not until I had remedied this deficiency, that I dared to feel his mental equal but out in the gardens, woods or shrubberies, I could always outclass him, much to his admiration, whatever game we chose to play.

For tonight's ball, I had a new, white and silver gown the most beautiful I had ever possessed, for Aunt Lucy had never made any difference between my wardrobe and that of her daughters.

From the very beginning, I had quickly come to the conclusion that Lady Perriman was an angel from heaven, so good towards me, but almost as quickly, I learned that she was a most unhappy woman. Lord Perriman very rarely came to visit her, preferring to stay in London where, being an intimate friend of the Prince of Wales, he led the gay life which Aunt Lucy had no wish to share.

I remember the first time I saw him. I had been at Perriman Court for about six months, when he unexpectedly turned up late one night. The next morning all the children, George, Mary, Barbara and little two-year-old Caroline had to present themselves in the library to greet Papa. I brought up the rear and stared with fascination at the big, handsome man wearing such gorgeous, colourful clothes, staring so hard that I almost forgot to make my curtsey as Martha had so emphatically instructed me to do.

As I hurriedly made my bob, he had laughed, loud and hearty, and had stepped forward, ignoring his own children, and had rumpled my short curls, which had now grown to a respectable length, doing away with any covering.

'A red-head, by God! You didn't tell me, My Lady, that this ward of yours was such a little beauty. She beats our brood into a frazzle.'

I saw the look of pain cross Lady

Perriman's face, but the next moment she was herself, smilingly, dismissing us. 'You may go now, children.'

'Yes, you may go, all but our little red-head. I've scarcely made her acquaintance. What is your name child?'

'Sophia Barton, sir.'

'Barton. Barton. I know quite a few Bartons . . . Which one do you come from?'

I didn't know what he meant, and looked towards Lady Perriman.

'Sophia knows but little of her parentage . . . '

'Ah — ah . . . a naughty little side-slip . . . '

For a moment Lady Perriman was silent. Then, 'No, Sir no. Sophy's parents were truly married . . . '

Dear, dear Lady Perriman. Always so ready to come to my rescue, even if she had to invent a white lie.

'La . . . spare me the boring details. One more brat in the household makes no difference. Upon my honour, she'll be a ravishing delight within a few years.'

'You may go, Sophia.' There was an unusual hardness in Aunt Lucy's voice and this time his Lordship made no attempt to stop me, but I could feel his eyes following me as I made a hasty curtsey and left the room.

After that, whenever he came up, he always appraised my looks, comparing me favourably with his daughters, and as the years slipped by, I sensed an attitude of being treated like a welcome guest.

There were occasions when he brought up some of his London cronies, and then the house and its mode of living was entirely transformed. There would be grand assemblies, when the ladies, painted and patched, with their hair dressed so ridiculously high, vied one with another in their gorgeous satin gowns, and display of sparkling jewels. The gentlemen were not to be left out, for in their peach-coloured waistcoats embroidered with silver and pearls, topped by jackets of vastly exaggerated cut, all added to the colourful scene.

Lady Perriman, as a truly dutiful wife, was the perfect hostess. Nor was she lacking when it came to being beautifully gowned. We children, under Martha's care, would peer over the banisters from the nursery landing, fascinated by the music and the dancers and the hundreds of gleaming, flickering candles. Yet for some strange reason, we were all glad when the house-party was over and Lord Perriman and his friends returned to London.

Last week he had sent word that he would not be coming up for George's farewell assembly, for with the expectancy of the Regency being declared any time now, His Highness the Prince of Wales could not spare his Lordship out of town. He would see his son in London before he sailed.

George had been jubilant when his mother had informed him. 'Three cheers for the Prince of Wales . . . and his Lordship. Hurrah! Hurrah! Hurrah!

'George!' His mother's voice was shocked. 'How can you be so discourteous to your father?'

'Don't pretend. Mama. You're as pleased as I am that he is not coming. He gives me a fit of the blue devils every time I am in his company.'

Now the last day had come. A marquee had been set up in the grounds where the guests could partake of refreshments and already the servants were setting out the tables. I got out of bed and standing at the window, watched their activities. I almost wished there had been no celebrations . . . just that we could have had George to ourselves on this his last day.

Martha came in, ostensibly to waken me and surprised to find me out of bed. Dear Martha, she was beginning to show signs of her age, but she refused to be pensioned off. 'I'd rather wear out, My Lady, than fall to pieces in rust,' she was fond of saying when urged to hand over some of her duties to the younger servants. I had much to thank Martha for. She it was who had taken me in hand, a pert chit if there ever was one; vulgar, ill-mannered and badly spoken. There had been many a scolding; many a sharp slap, but I had emerged, loving the old woman and now nearly twenty, grateful for her patience with such a difficult task.

'Lawks, Miss Sophie! I expected to find you dead to the world after your high jinks last night.'

'High jinks?' I queried innocently.

'I heard you and Master George . . .'

'And Miss Mary and Miss Barbara,' I added archly.

'And I know how late it was before you came to bed . . .'

'We were practising the new dances, Nannie, so that we can preen ourselves before the others tonight.' I made an exaggerated leg, and in a foppish drawl asked, 'Our dance, I believe, Miss Martha. Are you acquainted with the Stag Chase? Or do you prefer the Macaroni? Or the News from Denmark . . .'

'Away with you Miss Sophy. Such nonsense!'

'Nonsense? You come and watch tonight. You'll see it's no nonsense, but prodigious hard work.'

* * *

It was prodigious hard work all that day, for guests kept arriving and had to be entertained and fussed. Lady Perriman and George greeted them on arrival and then they were handed over to Mary and me to accompany them to their rooms, making sure they had everything they needed.

We couldn't resist having a giggle over some of the young ladies and their Mamas; they made it so obvious that they had high hopes of attracting George. Then as the day wore on, the tormenting thought grew within me; I didn't want George to even like any of these girls, let alone oh, no, he couldn't . . . he must not ask any of them . . . he must not ask their mamas . . . he was my dearest, very own George . . . he couldn't marry any of them.

As Martha brushed out my curls and twisted them round her finger to bring them to perfection, I calmed down. George would marry some day. Nothing was surer, but I need not pester myself, he was not yet nineteen, and he was being sent abroad. I had nothing to fear. I could relax. None of these young ladies had the remotest chance of being the next Lady Perriman . . . well not until he returned from India.

★ ★ ★

I don't think I ever saw Aunt Lucy look so beautiful as she did that night. Dancing was in the long, panelled portrait gallery, where former Perriman lords and their ladies looked down from their gilt frames; some with beauty and graciousness; some with haughty disdain. The gallery was crowded when the first band struck up for a minuet. I was with the family party and I watched and waited, my heart pounding with jealous fears as to who George would choose to partner him in the opening dance. From their painted faces, I could tell, all those powdered and patched big bosomed mamas along with their coy, simpering daughters, were experiencing the same anxiety. Then, joy oh joy, George turned to his mother and asked her for the honour, and they were on the floor alone; the dashing young officer and the proud, elegant gentlewoman, to whom I owed everything.

Her petticoat was of pale green quilted satin, richly embroidered with pink and silver spangles, while the overdress of delicate gauze was drawn up in festoons, with bunches of flowers. She looked so young under the blaze of candles that a stranger would never have guessed that George was her son, and that there were six other young Perrimans.

Mary, at seventeen, was a beauty; not with her mother's fragile flower-like looks, but a real dark-eyed, impetuous Perriman. Tonight, her betrothal to young Sir Henry Stainton was being announced and as they took the floor to join her mother and brother, I felt a touch of envy.

How would I find a husband, having no family and more to the point, no dowry; true, I always had a vast number of partners at any assembly I attended, but the gentlemen's interest soon waned when they discovered that I was but a penniless ward. What would happen next year, when twenty-one, free to leave Lady Perriman's service? No doubt, Aunt Lucy would ask me to stay, for over the years, I had been 'big sister' to the younger children and now two-year old Charles was the delight of my heart. There was a governess for Caroline, Sara and Elizabeth, but she was so intent on their schooling, that they always sought my company for their leisure hours.

No doubt, I could take a post as governess, for I had been an apt scholar but the thought of leaving Perriman Court filled me with misery.

We had to wait until Lady Perriman rejoined our party, before the gentlemen could ask her permission to be allowed to dance with us. Then there we were, out on the waxed floor, forgetting most of what our dancing masters had told us; just giving ourselves up to the intoxicating music and listening to the brash flattery of our partners.

George was quick to claim me for the next dance but in his arms, my heartache became intensified. The thought, that tomorrow, we were parting for several years, was almost unbearable, but I managed to keep smiling as though I was the happiest girl on the ballroom floor. It was as we were walking off at the end of the dance, that we noticed a footman in urgent conversation with Aunt Lucy.

'Poor Mama,' remarked George.

'She must be fatigued with all this organisation.'

Joining her, she looked at us with a troubled smile, ' 'Tis Charles, poor lamb. The excitement and staying up late has been too much for him. He's been sick and now he's screaming his head off. Martha fears he might have a fit with so much screaming. I must go to him.'

'I'll go Aunt Lucy. I can manage him better than Martha. I'll quieten him. You stay here.'

'But Sophy,' came George's expostulation. 'We're only waiting for the encore . . . you're my partner . . . '

'You'll easily find another. I'll be back for our second dance.'

'The devil you will or I'll come and fetch you . . . '

'Thank you Sophy,' Aunt Lucy's gentle voice cut in, 'I am indeed grateful but if you need me . . . '

Up in the night nursery, I found a very sad little boy but in my arms, his sobs gradually subsided. For a while,

I walked about with him crooning lullabies heedless of my ball-gown or his tiny, wet face against my cheek.

At last, I put him back into his crib. He didn't stir so, nodding to the nursery-maid, I tip-toed from the room and made my way downstairs.

It then occured to me that my face and hair might need attention before rejoining the assembly. Sitting down before my dressing table, I cooled my cheeks with angelwater and combed my curls into position, where Charles' tiny fingers had tangled them.

Coming out from my room, I almost collided with a tall, broad-shouldered gentleman looking about him in a most bewildered manner.

He bowed. 'Your pardon, ma'am. It would appear, I have lost my way. Lord Perriman himself, brought me up to my room to wash away the dust of our journey . . . now I would return to him in the library, I find myself lost in a labyrynth of corridors.'

I knew I should direct him, but all

I could stammer was, 'Lord Perriman? Here?'

He laughed; a genial, yet gentle laugh. 'Lady Perriman showed equal surprise . . . but there, ma'am, my manners are sorely lacking. Julian Masters at your service.'

' . . . and I am Sophia Barton, Lady Perriman's ward.'

'So you are Miss Barton? His Lordship has spoken much of you.'

I ignored the compliment. 'But what is his Lordship doing here? We did not expect him . . . '

'So I gather, but his Lordship and I have urgent business in Leeds tomorrow. We were almost there when Lord Perriman suddenly decided that as Perriman Court was not too far out of our way, we might as well stay there in comfort as in some flea-bitten hostelry. It was not until we heard the revelry that he recalled tonight was the occasion of his son's farewell assembly . . . hence our unexpected appearance.'

I felt a surge of anger that his Lordship could be so indifferent to George's departure but remembering that Mr. Masters was not to blame, I said quietly, 'We are accustomed to these surprises. His Lordship rarely notifies us of his intended visits. But now, sir, let me show you the way down. Are you going to join us in the ballroom?'

'Regretfully, no, ma'am. I am dressed but for travelling and in any case, it is our intention to be away early in the morning.'

By now, we had reached the main landing and Mr. Masters paused by the balustrade to look down on the brilliantly dressed throng cavorting and swaying to the lilt of the music, their silks and satins glowing under the blaze of the chandeliers while their jewels caught by the candle-light split up into myriads of facets of light.

For the first time I was able to take a good look at his face. I could not fathom the expression behind his eyes.

Talking to him, I had judged him to be easy-going and likeable. Now I saw a hard steel-like look in those eyes. Was it anger or scorn?

Joining him, I begged to be excused. As though he had not heard me, he indicated the dancers. 'This, Miss Barton, is of course, your accustomed world.'

I did not like the tone of his voice and was quick to retort in my iciest manner 'Yes sir. What of it?'

'You enjoy it?'

'Is there any reason why I should not?'

'That depends, ma'am, on whether you are aware of misery and poverty throughout the country . . .'

'Ah . . . so you are one of the reforming party . . . ?'

He laughed, once more a good-natured laugh. 'You are indeed perceptive, Miss Barton. Yes, I am a keen supporter of reform . . .'

'Then how come you to be friendly with Lord Perriman?'

'Could he too not favour reform?'

I shrugged my shoulders not knowing what to reply. How could his Lordship, an aristocrat, friend of the Prince of Wales be interested in reform?

He was still talking. 'Tomorrow we journey to Leeds to put into motion a project that we hope will give employment to several hundreds, men, women and children . . . '

'Children?' The solitary word escaped me as I recalled the sight of tired, weary children returning to the workhouse after several hours' labour in the mills, too tired to eat the miserable portion of food put before them.

I eyed him steadily. 'You favour reform . . . but not the abolition of child labour?'

'Miss Barton . . . may I say how much I admire your way of argument. Lord Perriman indeed spoke truly when he said you were a most unusual type of young lady. I too abhor child labour but their parents are only too glad of the extra pence they earn. Until they are given a living wage, their children will have to work.'

There was a chuckle of mirth behind us. 'I might have guessed. Is this rascal, Miss Sophy, filling your head with his fantastic reform ideas?'

Turning, I made a small curtsey to Lord Perriman, at the same time, expressing my pleasure at seeing him.

'Yes. 'Tis a pity we cannot stay, but now that we have joint interests up here in the North, you will be seeing much more of us.'

I dropped another curtsey of farewell to Mr. Masters who bowed low in return, but not so low that I did not fail to see the twinkle in his eye, ' . . . and when we do, Miss Barton, perhaps you will give me more of your views on child labour?'

As I made my way back to the ballroom, I was aware of my flushed cheeks. Was the man laughing at me, deriding women who took interest in politics? But back with George who was anxiously watching the big double doorway, I quickly forgot the impertinent Mr. Masters.

The dancing in the gallery and the feasting and drinking in the marquees went on into the early hours of the morning. Gradually, the mamas and papas and chaperones had to admit their weariness and call their carriages, or if staying in the house, wend their way to bed, but making sure their darling daughters went with them. Too many of the gentlemen had had too much to drink.

Aunt Lucy was one of the last to go, Barbara and Mary accompanying her. Seeing her weariness, I offered to stay a little longer to see to the needs of the dallying ladies, and was rewarded with one of her sweet smiles.

'Thank you, dear Sophy. George, look after her. She, too, must be fatigued.'

We sat and watched the few straggling dancers; commenting on the weariness of the musicians; the highlights and comic scenes of the evening, laughing together as we had done through our years of growing up.

Dawn was breaking as we waved to the last departing carriage, and going back into the house, we were struck by the eerie silence . . . everyone had gone. Then the silence was broken. Through the open door, we heard a bird call. Then another, and then more and more joined in the chorus, and I found George was holding my hand. There was a huskiness in his voice, 'Let's go outside, Sophy. It might be a long time before I hear another dawn chorus.'

To this day I can still bring back the perfume of those roses, dew-drenched, as we walked hand in hand between the massed beds and the canopies of climbers. Save for the scent and sound, I was almost unaware of anything else; unaware of where we were walking, until I found we were by the side of the lake and that George was no longer holding my hand, but had his arm around me.

'This was where it all began, Sophy . . . This is the proper place to begin another chapter . . . oh Sophy, dear, adorable little Sophy, I love you . . . I think I've always loved you . . . and I can't go away without telling you . . . without asking you . . . '

The unexpectedness of George's declaration threw my brain into confusion, but with returning sensibility, I managed to stammer.

'But George, you know my affection for you . . . '

'I don't want affection Sophy. I want you. I want your love . . . '

There was such urgency in his voice that I felt a moment of fear, but I quickly dismissed it. George would never hurt me . . . our friendship was too strong, but it was obvious he had had too much to drink. I took command, as I did in our childhood games.

'Listen, George. Don't spoil this wonderful evening, or rather this beautiful morning . . . '

'Then give me your promise, Sophy . . . that you will wait for me . . . that you will marry me . . . '

I wanted to protest, but he had drawn me to him and his lips were on mine, and then to my shame, glorious, heavenly shame, I was returning his caresses. No man had ever kissed me before and I felt as though my heart was being torn from my body. Then I broke away.

'George . . . this is madness . . . for both of us . . . '

'Yes, Sophy . . . it is madness . . . blissful . . . beautiful madness . . . Oh Sophy . . . beloved, say you love me . . . say it . . . you beloved little torment.'

'I love you George. Indeed I do . . . but . . . '

He laughed triumphantly and gathered me into his arms again. 'Say you'll wait for me, Sophy. Give me your promise to marry me . . . '

At first I couldn't find the words. Then, 'How can it ever be, George?

54

You are the Perriman heir ... I am a nobody.'

For a moment, I was tempted to tell him of my workhouse origin, but it seemed so far away and so ugly that I couldn't mar the beauty of the moment.

'Nonsense! You are the daughter of Mama's friend ... and what care I who you are? You are my own, beautiful little Sophy. Oh, Sophy, you must believe me. I've met scores of girls since I left home. None of them affected me in the least. You were always there ... '

'But George, your parents ... they would never consent ... '

'Why not? Mama adores you. My father has nothing but praise for you ... the few times he visits *The Court*. No darling ... I see no obstacle ... '

I shook my head. 'I wish I felt so sure. Your father will want you to make an advantageous marriage, a bride who can bring a handsome dowry ... '

He kissed me again. 'Don't argue,

my darling. By the time I return, I shall be of age. If there are any objections placed in our path, we'll elope . . . '

'That would be too unkind to your mother . . . '

'She will never object . . . '

'But . . . I am not a suitable person to be your wife. Some day you will be Lord Perriman.'

' . . . Then you will be Lady Perriman . . . '

I shook my head and was about to make another protest which he quickly silenced with a kiss.

'Give me your promise, Sophy . . . '

'On one condition . . . '

'Anything — you torment.'

'We keep the promise secret . . . for your mother's sake. While she might be friendly disposed towards me, I would not have her battling with your father. Besides, if the matter angered them, they could send me away.'

I saw at a glance that my last argument had convinced him. 'Very well, my love. But with this lovely morning, here at Perriman, as our witness, you are my promised wife.'

We kissed. Hard, long and passionate; a kiss to be remembered, heady with fumes of brandy and claret. Then with our arms entwined about each other, we walked slowly back towards the house.

'You will write often, my little love, telling me of the comings and goings of Perriman . . . and reassuring me of your love . . . '

'As often as you write to me,' I teased in a prim voice.

He groaned. 'I'm a complete ninny when it comes to writing letters. I can never command my thoughts into written words.'

'Practice will make perfect, sir,' I laughed.

'But seriously, dear heart. If my letters sound stilted . . . barren . . . you will understand?'

I smiled up at him, so young and handsome; once the playmate of my childhood; now my avowed lover.

'You and I have always understood each other, George . . . always been able to say what was in our minds and in our hearts.'

He was kissing me again; then resting his face against my cheek, his voice came low, 'Sophy. There is something I want to say to you . . . something which I cannot say to anyone else.'

I released myself, so that I could look him in the face.

'Do you think you should confide in me . . . surely . . . '

'Who else? You are my nearest and dearest. Oh God, Sophy! How I hate the army! Just because the Perriman heir has always held a commission . . . I too am forced into it!'

'Oh George! George! That you should be unhappy!'

'You know what we have talked of . . . All I wanted to do was to work for the betterment of Perriman. To improve the estate . . . new ideas for its prosperity . . . to improve the condition of our workers . . . '

I tried to soothe him. 'When you come home, George . . . '

'When! You mean 'if'!'

'George . . . don't say such things! Don't think them.'

His arms enclosed me once again. 'But I do think about them . . . all the time. I am afraid, Sophy. Not so much of being killed . . . that would be a definite end . . . but of being maimed . . . of becoming fever-ridden . . . the long, long absence from home . . . away from you . . . my whole future seems so clouded.' He paused for a moment, then added mockingly, 'But a Perriman must never show fear.'

Gently I kissed him, and it struck me oddly that the kiss was like that of a mother consoling a disappointed child.

'It is not fear,' I whispered. 'Just the disappointment that all your plans are being delayed. The time will pass quickly. Strange, interesting places. New friends . . . '

'And the everlasting, pestering thought, that you too will have other admirers.

59

You will be true to me. Sophy? You will wait for me?'

We had reached the house. We stopped before going through the door. I had almost reached the limit of my endurance, for only too well I knew of the dangers he would have to face, and I, too, was full of fear and foreboding. All the glory of our passion by the lake-side seemed to have receded; a melancholy sweetness taking its place.

'Have no fear, George. All will be well . . . and I will always love you.' He drew me to him, but even as he kissed me, I tore myself away, for the tears were so dangerously near. Without looking back, I dashed into the house.

Taking off my ball-gown, I threw myself upon the bed, but sleep would not come, my mind being so bemused; elated by George's passionate kisses, melancholy at the thought of his so-near departure; fearful for both our futures. I had given him my promise, but how binding was it, with such a disparity between our positions . . . and our ages, for in that first passionate kiss, I had sensed my maturity . . . my power to dominate, even exploit the situation had I so wished. And George? To me he was still the play-mate of my childhood . . . not yet ready for marriage or even a serious contract . . . and in three year's time he might see the affair in a totally different light.

* * *

All the family and household staff gathered to wave God-speed to the young master. He kissed his mother and sisters, Baby Charles . . . and Martha . . . then finally, I too received a gentle farewell embrace, only his hand, gripping mine so tightly that I winced with the pain, spoke of his love. Then, lest the emotion that I could see was mounting within him became too apparent, he hurriedly got into the carriage . . . and it was moving away . . . the horses quickly gathering speed, and then I felt such a sense of loss as I would never have believed possible . . . a sense of foreboding that a beautiful part of my life had come to an end . . . not the beginning.

2

With George's departure, an air of depression seemed to settle over the Court, so alien to it's usual quiet bustle, Aunt Lucy appearing more grieved than I had ever known her. Where there are children, however, despondency never lasts long and Baby Charles, who everyone adored soon had us back in our normal good spirits.

Between George and Charles, there were five girls, three still in the schoolroom, Barbara just emerging and Mary soon to be a bride.

Up to about four years ago, we had more or less, lived in a small world of our own but with George bringing friends, from the military college and Mary rapidly becoming a young lady, Aunt Lucy had begun to entertain on a wider scale. Consequently, in return, there was a steady stream of invitations from all over the county, invitations that always included me . . . otherwise declined by her Ladyship. How welcome they were now, to relieve the tedium of waiting. Waiting for what?

There had been a brief letter from George written just before he sailed, merely relating how his father had taken him around London . . . to his club . . . to the theatre . . . a letter I was able to show Aunt Lucy and the others . . . but not the slip of paper bearing the words, 'I love you, I adore you. George . . .'

I didn't like this secrecy about our love, but after all, it had been my idea. Although I loved George, each night as I composed myself for sleep, praying for his safety, I would ask myself the same question. Dare I marry him?

I took to walking in the woods alone, communing with myself, turning questions over in my mind, but always coming back to the same point. There was such a strong bond between us . . . not that I had saved his life . . . but that his childhood companionship and his ready acceptance of me . . . a stranger . . . had given me a new life.

Aunt Lucy and Martha both remarked on my abstraction and decided we all needed a change. Although now September, the weather was still warm; we would go to Scarborough, taking the children. They were hilarious with delight, but not so Mary, for although Scarborough in the north ranked equally with Brighton, both as to sea bathing and high society, she had a much different idea. Why couldn't we go to London? George's description of the capital had whetted her appetite. Papa had a huge mansion in the Mall, scarcely ever occupied. It would be so much more advantageous to buy her trousseau and linen in London . . . more selection . . . the latest ton. It was really most unfair of Mama keeping us buried alive here in Yorkshire, just because she didn't like high society life. We could visit the theatres . . . the pleasure gardens . . . London life must be wonderful. I, too, was thrilled at the idea and waited with bated breath for Aunt Lucy's reply. She never went to London, detesting, she said, the outrageous behaviour of its society.

Imagine our delight, when the next day, she told us that she had already written to his Lordship, but in the meantime, while awaiting his reply, we should go with the children to Scarborough and see them settled in the villa.

It was a newly built house standing in its own grounds not far from the sea. Every morning, each one of us, including Aunt Lucy, with a retinue of nursery-maids, went down to the sea-shore, where we had our own private bathing machines. Undressing in the window-less little huts on wheels and putting on our grey flannel, all enveloping bathing dresses, we then stood swaying from side to side, as

Perriman horses, specially trained for the job, dragged our bathing machines out into the sea.

Not until we were well away from all male-prying eyes, was the door opened and we tremulously picked our way down the wooden steps. As we gingerly trod the water, we thought ourselves so brave, until one of the waiting dippers seized us and plunged us into the sea, right over our heads, before lifting us out spluttering with mixed terror and enjoyment. Little did the others know, that each time I was dipped, I was back in the workhouse-shack, scared and trembling, hearing the raucous laughter of Mrs. Mathews and Mrs. Needler.

In the evening there were assemblies and balls, and Mary, Barbara and I, chaperoned by Aunt Lucy, had our share of the fun, but we were all too excited by the prospect of our London visit to really appreciate it.

Then came word that, although His Lordship was at present staying at the

Royal Pavillion in Brighton, he would endeavour to visit us, while we were in town, and take us to the theatre.

We couldn't get back to the Court quickly enough, to pack and be on our way, leaving the children with an army of nurses and servants, sworn by Her Ladyship to watch over them with the greatest of care.

We were almost in London, having passed through a number of pretty little villages, which we had been informed, made up outer London. I think it was the smell ... the hot, fetid smell, that made us aware when we were in the capital itself. As we each screwed up our noses, Mary sharply closed the window near where she was sitting, bidding Barbara do the same on her side. Groups of dirty, ill-clad men and women, and almost naked children looked up from where they were sprawling by the roadside, shouting unintelligible insults at us as our carriages rattled over the cobbles.

'Why are they shouting at us?' asked Barbara.

Aunt Lucy shrugged her shoulders. 'You will see many people like them in London. They are poor . . . and hungry.'

'But that is not our fault!'

'No? Then whose fault is it? You will also see such unbelievable extravagance amongst Papa's friends . . . '

'Then blame Papa and his friends! Perhaps the Prince of Wales himself!' interrupted Mary.

'Whoever is to blame, there is nothing that we, as women can do. If we were to try to dispense charity here, as we do at *Perriman*, they would most likely set about us, and tear us to pieces.'

Barbara shuddered. 'I don't think I'm going to like it here in London . . . '

'You'll be safe enough, child, in the carriage with a strong coachman and groom, and two footmen, but you must not attempt to walk out alone . . . remember!'

I had not joined in the conversation

for my sympathies were with those poor creatures by the roadside, outside the hovels they called home. Since I had become of an age when I could reason things out for myself, I had realised that there were but two classes of human beings, the rich . . . and the poor . . . and the rich, save but for a few, cared naught for the poor . . . and the poor . . . save but for a few, could see no way to appease their hunger, squalor and misery, except by violence.

In that moment, as we approached *Perriman House*, a huge square building, standing back behind tall, iron railings, I knew that somehow, sometime, I must endeavour to do something for these poor wretches. They were my kind.

★ ★ ★

The major domo was waiting for us. Bowing deeply to Lady Perriman, he quickly instructed waiting maids to take us up to our rooms, giving us no time to look around the vast, marble hall with its galaxy of thick, richly coloured oriental rugs.

We exclaimed in delight as we walked into our bedrooms . . . a room for each one of us, with Martha and Lady Perriman's maid, Dorcas, sharing a room next to their mistress.

Young Dorcas sniffed significantly as she came to unpack for me. 'Good to tell, Miss Sophy, that 'tisn't long since these rooms were occupied . . . and by women.'

I was quick on the defensive. 'Lord Perriman places his town house at the disposal of many of his friends . . . and their families,' but deep down I wondered just who the last occupants had been, and what they meant to his Lordship, especially the occupant of Lady Perriman's room.

They were truly feminine bedrooms; the curtains and bed-hangings being of delicate pastel shaded satin, and the chairs and sofas covered in striped damask. On the dressing-tables was an assortment of creams, skin-washes, hair powder and perfume, most of which we had never before heard of. Back home, Aunt Lucy allowed us to use some cosmetics and toilet waters, such as honey-water, Imperial water and the lovely eau-de-cologne. Sniffing curiously at some of the pastes and pomatums, we found they were truly foul-smelling, which Martha advised us to leave alone; seeing that they contained acids which would do our skin more harm than good . . . as for some of them . . . if we knew from what they were made, we would turn up our noses in disgust!

We dined quietly that night, and after wandering through the house, which was furnished in a much more modern style than *Perriman Court*, we retired early, tired and excited.

My room was the farthest away from Lady Perriman's on the corner of the house, giving me wide, uninterrupted views. Just where was *Carlton House*?

Drury Lane Theatre? Covent Garden? The shops? Vauxhall? Ranehalgh? I fell asleep, dreaming of richly attired ladies and gentlemen, parading the streets, bowing low to me as I strutted along.

★ ★ ★

We spent most of the next morning at Madame Triaud's in Bond Street, choosing the material and style for Mary's wedding dress. Never before had I realised that such beautiful silks and satins existed; but there I was, also being measured for my bridesmaid's gown . . . choosing my own material.

There were other shops to visit; the linen mercer's . . . the furrier's . . . the jeweller's . . . even the toy-shops to take gifts back for the children. Despite the risk of having stones thrown at our carriage, we had the hood down, so that we could see the sights; our footmen standing behind; their canes in readiness.

The streets and parks were thronged

with people, some riding in their carriages; others walking, the ladies timorously holding their escort's arm.

We pulled up outside Westminster Abbey, to admire its beauty . . . to listen to Barbara and Mary, painting a picture of the next coronation, which their parents would be commanded to attend. Aunt Lucy made a wry face, but had to laugh at Mary's description of her long velvet robes and coronet, complete with page boy. Little Charles?

Then we drove slowly past *Carlton House*, the Prince of Wales' London residence.

'When I am married, Papa says that Henry and I will be invited to dine with the Prince.' Mary's voice was full of arrogance.

Barbara's eyes opened wide. 'Really? Could we not be invited now, Mama?'

'The Prince is in Brighton. No doubt if he were in residence we should be, for he thinks highly of your Papa.'

'Then why do we not visit London more often? I should so adore to move in Royal society.' Barbara spoke wistfully.

'Papa says Henry and I can have use of his London house whenever we wish . . . so you must come too, Barbara.'

Aunt Lucy laughed. 'As a young bride, you will not wish to chaperone your sister. Maybe, like me, you will soon tire of the everlasting round of dinners and assemblies, card playing parties, gossiping and back-biting, for that is the chief occupation of London society.'

'Oh, no, no,' chorused both girls. 'We all ought to live more in London, don't you think so, Sophy?'

Until now, I had taken no part in the conversation. It seemed so utterly ridiculous to think of me being presented to the Prince of Wales — Sophia Barton, the most impudent little bastard from a certain Lancashire institution.

I had to laugh at my imagination. 'Of a certainty, I am enjoying every moment, but whether it would eventually pall, I cannot tell.'

'When do you think Papa will visit us?' Barbara's voice was anxious. 'I'm so longing to go to a theatre.'

'That is more than I can say,' was Aunt Lucy's abrupt answer, so you can guess the excitement when, on returning to Perriman House, we found that Lord Hugh had arrived, and was in the library awaiting us.

He greeted Aunt Lucy courteously, kissing her on both cheeks, but there was much more exhuberance than usual in his welcome for his daughters.

'Now with you two pretty things here, the house looks like coming alive for once. And Sophy! And what do you think of London city?'

He kissed me warmly, as became a guardian, while I thought out a reply. 'So far, sir, we have seen but little of it.'

'Well then, by God, that's something we must remedy. Tonight we'll go to the theatre. We have a box at Drury Lane. Then for tomorrow,

I've already invited a crowd from Brighton. We'll show 'em just how the Perrimans can entertain . . . the finest assembly London has seen these last few months.'

Barbara and Mary clapped their hands in glee. 'Have you invited the Prince of Wales, Papa?' Barbara asked breathlessly.

'I asked him, sweet, but he sent his apologies . . . He's almost crippled with gout . . . '

Was it imagination that I saw a look of relief pass over Aunt Lucy's face? But with Lord Hugh's next words, I saw the relief overtaken by consternation . . . 'but he has asked me to take you all back with me to Brighton . . . '

'Oh Papa! Papa! How wonderful! When do we go?'

'I shall have to talk that over with your mother . . . '

'We can go, Mama, can we not?'

'One thing at a time, Barbara. We are going to the theatre tonight . . . tomorrow we are giving an assembly . . . I doubt that we have brought sufficient or grand enough gowns for Brighton . . . '

'But Papa will give us money for more . . . will you not, Papa?'

'Assuredly . . . my girls must be the belles of the ball, wherever they go . . . '

'Then, Mama . . . say it is settled . . . '

Aunt Lucy's voice was cold. 'Go up to your rooms girls. There is much that I must talk over with your father.'

I knew then that we should not be going to Brighton. I could tell by the tone of Aunt Lucy's voice . . . the inscrutable look on her face. We each made a quick curtsey and left the room.

Mary, too, had sensed her mother's antagonism to the idea of visiting Brighton.

'Truly, I'm sorry for you two poor creatures, but for my part, I prefer not to be presented until I am married, and Henry accompanies me . . . '

'Why should Mama be such a spoilsport?' Barbara could hardly keep back the tears. ' . . . when Papa is so anxious to take us?'

Martha, having already been informed of Lord Hugh's arrival, and guessing that we should be entertaining to being entertained, was already hanging our gowns about the room, so that they would be creaseless by the time we wanted to wear them.

For some reason or other, we girls dined upstairs in our rooms, Barbara and Mary arguing between themselves as to the cause. Were their parents indulging in a violent quarrel . . . or could it be that Mama had mellowed a little and she and papa were enjoying a tête-a-tête meal? As usual I kept out of the discussion. I loved Aunt Lucy. Whatever she did, was right in my eyes.

It was to Drury Lane that Lord Hugh took us, and as we entered the theatre, we were met by Mr. Sheridan himself. I found his effusion most amusing, and it took me all my time to keep a straight face when, along with everyone else, I was presented to him, before being taken into our box.

Lord Perriman was most attentive, seeing to it that we had the seats giving the best views of the stage, he being quite content to remain in the background. 'I've seen this play many times before . . . You'll enjoy it.'

'What is it Papa?'

'*The Country Girl*, with Dorothy Jordan taking the lead . . . '

'Isn't she getting rather old for the part?' interrupted Aunt Lucy rather quickly.

Lord Hugh shrugged his shoulders. 'When she begins to act, you forget her age.'

'Papa?' It was Barbara again. 'Those ladies . . . down in the front row . . . wearing very low dresses . . . and lots of paint and patches . . . ?'

A look of amusement crossed her father's handsome face. 'Those, dear child, are certain ladies of the town and they pay an extra high price for their front-row seats.'

'But why, Papa?'

'That is enough Barbara. Please cease staring in that direction.' Aunt Lucy tapped her on the arm with her fan. 'We don't want them staring up at us.'

Indeed it seemed to me that at that moment, everybody was staring about them, across at other boxes or down into the pit. Our box was very near the stage and directly opposite, the sole occupant of another box seemed very interested in us. The light from the candles was too flickering to get other than a blurred view of his face, but when, before sitting down, he gave us a courteous bow, I realised to my horror, I had been staring at him and that it was Mr. Masters!

How thankful I was that he was too far away to see my rising colour.

The orchestra was now playing 'The King' and for the first time in my life, I felt a stir of patriotism. That all these people should rise to their feet and sing with such enthusiasm . . . there must be something in being an English citizen.

The candles were snuffed and the curtains drawn back. Slowly, scarcely realising it. I found myself being transported to another world . . . a world of glamorous unreality . . . the world of theatre and make-believe. How I envied those graceful creatures flitting about the stage. What fortunate, happy people they must be!

Then I was unceremoniously jerked back into reality, as Dorothy Jordan made her entrance.

I felt a surge of disappointment. She was fat. Not just plump . . . but fat. Then she laughed. Perhaps, I thought, she's laughing at herself for being so fat . . . but the laughter was so sweet, so mellow, so heartwarming, that I instinctively knew her to be tender and loving and generous. Now the audience was laughing with her. I couldn't understand all her jokes, but

I gathered they must be bawdy judging by the hearty laughter of the grown-ups. Then she sang . . . her voice as luscious as her laughter . . . and as she gestured and moved about the stage, the whole audience appeared to forget that she was a middle-aged, fat . . . woman.

There were other actors and actresses too; all of who appeared to me as creatures from another world . . . a world denied to ordinary people, but then, too soon the play was ended and reluctantly we were going down to our waiting carriage.

It was as Lord Hugh was handing me in, that I saw Julian Masters once again, smilingly watching us, or I conceitedly asked myself, was he watching me? Behind Lord Hugh's back, he gave me the slightest of mocking bows but not before I had got a full glimpse of his young, good-looking face. Had he seen my confusion, I wondered, as I hastily took my place?

This time, it was Mary being inquisitive. 'That actress, Dorothy Jordan, is she not the mistress of the Duke of Clarence?'

'She is . . . but none the less, a good woman. She is most highly thought of in the Royal Circle,' came her father's quick, curt answer.

'Then why does he not marry her?' demanded Barbara.

'Because the Royal Marriage Act forbids marriage between Royalty and a commoner. 'T'would seem, ma'am,' he went on, turning to Aunt Lucy, 'the education of our daughters is progressing.

Back home we couldn't go straight to bed. We had so much to talk about, so the three of us, with cups of hot chocolate, sat around my fire, well into the early hours, until Martha broke up the party, reminding us of the full day before us on the morrow . . . more shopping . . . more sight-seeing and a visit to the hairdressers. But I couldn't sleep. I was back at Drury Lane . . . up on the stage . . . singing . . . dancing . . . for my voice had responded well to tuition while the dancing master was for ever praising my lightness. Supposing . . . just supposing . . . I wished to leave Aunt Lucy when I was twenty-one . . . could I . . . would I be worthy of a place on the stage . . . to entertain people? Then I realized the absurdity of it all. I was going to marry George. I was promised to him. Yet both my past and my future were so wrapped by dark, impenetrable clouds that I found it impossible to imagine myself as his wife. Marriage to him could occasion a family upheaval, perhaps disruption. Dare I risk it? Did we love each other enough to stand up against the world? More important still, was I really in love with him? Surely if I were, I should have no doubts about the future. Yet, I knew I longed to experience those heady passionate kisses again, aching with the thought of at least two empty, barren years. Was George suffering in the same way? Did men suffer from the pangs of love? I knew so little of love or men . . . and there was no-one to whom I could turn for advice.

3

We were down for breakfast quite early, remembering Aunt Lucy had ordered the carriage for noon, only to be informed by Martha there was no hurry as His Lordship and Lady Perriman were closeted in the library with the family lawyer.

We looked at each other in bewilderment, till Barbara asked, 'What do you think they are talking about?'

'How should I know?' was Mary's waspish retort, 'All I do know is there will be little time to choose new gowns.'

'Perhaps it concerns your dowry,' came the helpful suggestion.

'Rubbish. That was settled months ago.' Despite Mary's cross voice, we were both totally unprepared for Barbara's sudden outburst of tears.

'Oh my God. What have I said

now? Really, Barbara, you should have stayed at Scarborough with the other children . . . '

'It must have been right what I heard Dorcas telling one of the housemaids . . . '

'If you've been listening to servants' gossip, you may as well tell us . . . '

'She . . . she said . . . she said, she'd heard Papa was seeking a legal separation . . . '

'Oh no . . . no . . . ' Both Mary and I spoke in unison but both our voices trailed away without qualifying our denial. We knew only too well the unhappy state between them.

When Mary spoke again, her voice was more gentle. 'You should never believe stupid servants' talk. I'd like to gamble they're discussing buying a town house for Henry and me . . . '

I was not so easily reassured. What would happen to me if there was a separation? I could hardly see that it would make any difference to Aunt Lucy's mode of living. She had money of her own, but she might vacate *Perriman Court*. I shook myself. How could she? It was the home of seven young Perrimans, and she was their mother. Lord Hugh would never be so cruel.

When at last the lawyers took their departure, I gave a sigh of relief, as I noted the good humour of His Lordship and the friendly smile of Aunt Lucy. Nothing drastic could have taken place, but we all felt much put out when told that, owing to the lateness of the hour, a visit to the shops was out of the question; we would have to make do with the gowns we had worn for George's leave-taking. Mary and Barbara immediately went off into a fit of the blue-devils, railing against their Mama, who should have forseen this eventuality.

In fact we didn't go out all that day; Lady Perriman instructing that hairdressers should be brought to the house much to Dorcas' indignation.

To this day, my memories of that

assembly stand out crystal clear. My first view of Lord Hugh and Aunt Lucy, ready to receive their guests; he so handsome and charming; she so beautiful and gentle. We girls took our places alongside them.

It was really laughable the way some of the men stared and ogled us; men wearing outrageous, foppish, tight-fitting clothes and monstrous high wigs, while the women with still more fantastic hair-styles wore gowns cut so low as to be almost indecent. When the men favoured Lady Perriman with exaggerated 'legs' and flourishes, the women eyed her almost malevolently.

I was so absorbed watching their antics, that I almost jumped when I heard the stentorian voice of the major-domo announcing 'Mr. Julian Masters.' Having heard nothing but a string of impressive titles it was odd to hear a name without one. Then I was aware of my pounding heart and the tightness in my throat as I watched his leisurely ascent of the grand staircase.

Lord Perriman stood by, smiling amicably as his guest greeted first Aunt Lucy, Mary and Barbara and then confronting me with that impertinent smile, bent low and kissed my finger-tips. Nothing more, for he immediately turned back for further chit-chat with his host. Obviously he was a close acquaintance of his Lordship . . . but no title!

From out of the hum of laughing conversation, came Lord Hugh's drawl, 'Sophia. I'm putting you in Mr. Master's care.' I felt my colour rising, as with the same teasing smile, the gentleman offered his arm to take me into dinner, remarking. 'So we meet again, Miss Sophia.'

'Yes, sir. The third time is it not?'

'And what is the saying? The third time pays for all.'

'Exactly what does that mean sir?'

He shrugged his shoulders laughingly. 'Whatever interpretation, you wish, Miss Sophia.'

He was I told myself, the most

handsome man at the assembly. To begin with, he wore no wig and after a surfeit of wigs and powder, his dark, naturally waved hair entranced me. His clothes were of excellent cut. Although they were marked by the absence of excessive frills and fripperies, favoured by dandies, he looked their equal in every way. Equal? No. Their superior.

My arm through his, was held tightly to his side; the feeling of security and of protection sending a thrill of ecstasy through my bemused mind.

As we waited to be served, I ventured, 'This is my first London assembly. 'Tis all too overwhelming.'

'You overwhelmed, Miss Sophia? Nothing could overwhelm you.'

'What makes you think that, sir?'

Again that tantalising smile. 'Your eyes. So calm and steady. 'Tis I who am overwhelmed, Miss Sophia, though not by the assembly but by . . . '

I knew what he was going to say. Other men had paid me similar flattering compliments and I was quick to stop him. 'This will be only one of the many assemblies you attend . . . '

' . . . It is my first at Perriman House . . . '

'Then you and Lord Hugh are not long acquainted?'

'A matter of a few months beginning as business associates but now . . . '

' . . . You have become friends?'

He regarded me steadily. 'Yes . . . we have become friends . . . as I hope we shall become . . . '

Again the feeling of trepidation . . . a feeling of joy . . . a strange, new joy.

The meal was now in progress but I was not aware of what I was eating. I was too engrossed listening to the man by my side. As I toyed with my food, I felt that I wanted the meal to go on and on, lest when it was over, I should never again see Julian Masters.

Then I heard music coming from the gallery. Of a certainty he would ask me to dance! Intoxicated by the music, we would be spirited away, forgetting all others, beginning with finger-tips just touching, hands gently clasped and our faces brought so dangerously near as we circled each other.

It was Lady Perriman's voice, suggesting that the ladies should retire to the drawing-room that brought me back with a start and as I shook my silly senses, I went into a further tizzy at Mr. Masters' whispered, 'My dancing, is but of poor quality, but will you please save two for me?'

★ ★ ★

Mary, Barbara and I had been instructed that we would be be expected to play and sing and as we were all reasonably proficient we knew we would give satisfaction but I felt so elated and excited that I performed as never before.

Aunt Lucy beamed her delight but it was obvious that few of the other ladies wished to be entertained, their strident voices drowning both our singing and the harpsichord. Accordingly, she motioned to us to close the instrument and turned to join in the conversation as became a good hostess.

What a tiresome long time the gentlemen took over their port but at last they joined us, choosing their partners for the first dance and drifting from the room.

Lord Perriman and Mr. Masters were the last to arrive, still in deep, earnest conversation but at the sight of us waiting, they quickly came over, both apologising most profoundly.

I rejoiced when Mr. Masters so courteously offered his arm to Aunt Lucy. I wanted her to like him and the manner in which he asked Lord Hugh if he might have the first dance with her Ladyship, filled me with pleasure. Not so, however, when for the next dance, he led Mary out on to the floor and I was positively raging, when, returning her, he asked Barbara to be his next partner! How could he do that to me? When some outrageously dressed macaroni sought Aunt Lucy's permission to partner me, I went out and danced with as much abandon as I could muster, returning haughty stares whenever I met Julian Masters' twinkling eyes.

When I rejoined our party, he was already there and lost no time in approaching me. Petulantly, I excused myself. I was too exhausted. Then would I give him the pleasure of being allowed to sit out with me? Or a walk in the garden? I couldn't resist his roguish smile. I had to capitulate and as we left the hot stuffy gallery, he again took my arm and put it through his, remarking, 'You were jealous, Miss Sophia! Now confess!'

I tried to remove my arm but it was impossible so I had to content myself with a scornful, 'Jealous! Why should I be jealous. Miss Mary is betrothed and Miss Barbara barely out of the schoolroom.' Then I looked up and caught his laughing eyes. 'All right, I confess. I was jealous. Now are you satisfied, sir?'

I felt an extra pressure on my arm as he replied, 'Indeed, yes, Miss Sophia for that tells me that at least you find me tolerable and now . . . where shall we go?'

I shrugged my shoulders. 'As yet, sir, I do not know the geography of either the house or garden . . . '

'Nor I, but I am assured that Lord Perriman had some truly magnificent tropical plants in his conservatory. Shall we discover it together?'

Although the heat in the conservatory was equally over-bearing as in the gallery it was at least almost deserted and we had no difficulty in finding a couple of cane chairs, Mr. Masters apparently no more interested in tropical plants than I was.

'If I told you I had a good reason for asking Miss Mary and Miss Barbara before you, would you believe me?'

'Of a certainty, sir . . . '

'Bless you for that, Miss Sophia. The truth is that I must leave the assembly early . . . '

'Oh no!' I was unable to keep back my disappointment. Then to cover my confusion, I went on, 'Of course, you must have many calls upon your time . . . a wide circle of friends . . . '

'Nothing of the kind, Miss Sophia. Throughout tonight, I drive down to Dover to catch tomorrow's channel crossing. As I told you at dinner, I am a shipping merchant; exporting English cloths; importing foreign silks. I go to France to buy silks.' As I made no reply, he went on, 'Etiquette will not allow me more than two dances with you so I schemed that I should take those two just prior to my departure . . . ' His voice was very low, ' . . . so that I should take away with me, the memory of you.'

I didn't know how to reply. No man had ever moved me in this way. No man had ever spoken to me with such sincerity.

'I . . . I think we should be getting back to the ball-room . . . '

'On my return, may I call on you?'

'By that time, sir, we may have returned to Yorkshire . . . '

'Then may I call on you in Yorkshire?'

'With Lady Perriman's permission, I shall be delighted.'

I tried to sound unconcerned, but already, I was wondering how long it would be before I saw him again.

There was amusement in his voice. 'Both Lord and Lady Perriman have already invited me to call whenever I am in Yorkshire . . . '

'You've been teasing me, sir. That was most unkind . . . '

'I like to see you in all your moods, Miss Sophia . . . so as to remember you in different ways . . . ' There was an urgency in his voice. I was suddenly afraid. Not of him but of myself . . . my low birth that sooner or later would have to be told, if . . . I shook myself. Men made pretty speeches to any and every woman who happened to catch their passing fancy.

'Really, sir, Lady Perriman will be growing flurried . . . and . . . and we should put in an appearance for the next dance.'

As we entered the gallery, we were hailed by Lord Hugh.

'Just the very two we need for this quadrille.' It was indeed a family affair save for the two young men partnering Mary and Barbara and as we danced, first one figure and then another, I was convinced that never before had I been so elated.

Then Julian Masters was taking his leave. As he kissed my hand, I dare not look up at him, fearing the others would read my telltale eyes. When he had gone, I felt so lost. So alone.

Aunt Lucy found more partners for us, but when we refused to stroll in the garden with them, they very ungallantly lost all interest in us, and there we were, truly wilting wallflowers.

As the night wore on, more and more ladies passed out with the heat; more and more gentlemen passed out with the drink so that in almost every room, male and female forms were stretched out on the sofas . . . dead to the world.

We would have said a formal goodnight to Lord Hugh, but the footmen, loyal to a man, vowed that they could not find him anywhere so Aunt Lucy bade us go to our beds but that she must remain until the last guest had gone.

Martha was waiting for us and I vow I saw a gleam of triumph in her eyes as she listened to our indignant outpourings about the behaviour of certain people.

'After that display, I have no wish to go to Brighton nor do I wish to go to another assembly without Henry's protection,' came Mary's emphatic denunciation.

'So London society isn't all you hoped it to be?' Martha's query held a note of scorn. 'Perhaps now, you can see why your Mama avoids it . . . '

'But Papa enjoys it,' wailed Barbara and then added mischievously, ' . . . and so does Sophia. She had an admirer tonight.'

'An admirer?' Martha's eyebrows were raised as she looked across at me. ' . . . and who might he have been?'

'La. Nanny. Don't pester yourself. He was of no consequence. A mere business-man. A shopkeeper.' Mary's voice was scornful.

'He is not a shopkeeper!' I was surprised at the vehemence in my voice. 'He is a . . . a . . . '

'Well, go on. Tell us about him. You were long enough in his company. You cannot deny he has no title.'

'Is a title so important?'

'Ah . . . then you are partial to him? Better not let Papa or Mama know . . . '

'He and Lord Perriman are great friends . . . '

'That does not signify. Papa is like the Prince of Wales. Both choose strange friends . . . '

'Did he declare himself?' giggled Barbara.

'Don't talk such nonsense!' Martha's

voice was full of irritation, ' . . . and with all these queer people around, remember to put chairs behind your doors.'

Barbara had to have the last word. 'Well, I swear here and now, that the man I marry, most certainly must have a title.'

★ ★ ★

For a long time, sleep evaded me, my excited brain reliving my brief time with Julian Masters. Though secretly betrothed to George, could I have fallen in love with this fascinating man? I was so naive. What was love? I only knew that my lips were hungry for hard-pressed kisses; my body yearning for breathtaking embraces, whether they were from George or Julian Masters. How low had I sunk. Was my wantoness a legacy from my mother?

I don't know whether I had actually been asleep or just dozing but suddenly

I was wide awake with the knowledge there was someone outside my bedroom door. I sat up and listened. Yes, the same bumping sound against the door; the same muttering and heavy breathing. Was someone ill? Forgetting my fears, I slipped out of bed and without stopping to put on a wrapper, I moved the chair from under the knob and opened the door.

The only light, was that which came from solitary candles left burning in the hall and occasional shafts of moonlight, but it was enough to show that my visitor was Lord Hugh. He almost fell into the room, still muttering, but at the sight of me standing there, in my thin nightrobe, he made an attempt to straighten himself, and closed the door.

'My little, Sophy. My dear, delicious little Sophy. Light the candle . . . so that I can see you the better.'

He was terribly, horribly drunk, reeking of wine and vomit.

'Sir. You must go . . . You have come

to the wrong room. Her Ladyship's room . . . '

'I don't want her Ladyship's room.' His speech was thick and maudlin. 'I want yours, Sophy. Only yours.'

In the eerie, moonlit room, I saw his arms reach out to take me. I dodged aside, and as I eluded him, he fell sprawling over a sofa.

He cursed loudly. 'Sir,' I begged. 'You must get out of here. Someone will hear you. Then . . . Then I shall be ruined.'

'Come and sit here with me Sophy . . . on this sofa . . . ' He gave a silly, stupid laugh, 'Sophy . . . sofa.'

By now I had found my wrapper, and felt more capable of dealing with the situation. But how? What could I do? In the darkness, I tried to think.

Then he rose to his feet and his arms were around me, and the next moment I was beside him on the sofa, my mouth crushed to his, being repeatedly kissed with violent passion. Struggle as I would, I could not free myself.

I dare not call out, lest I awaken the household. Who would believe my story against his Lordship's?

At last his hold around me slackened, his heavy breathing became less laboured, as he attempted to talk.

'Don't struggle so, my lovely little Sophy. I want you. I want you more than I have ever wanted any other woman. When I saw all those others tonight with their greedy, lecherous eyes upon you, I knew. I was jealous. Come to me, Sophy. You shall want for nothing. Money . . . jewels . . . they shall be yours.'

'Sir, you don't know what you're talking about. The rooms have been too hot and you have had too much wine. Let me take you to Lady Perriman's room . . .'

There was derision in his laughter. ' . . . and do you think her Ladyship would thank you? No. I stay with you, my lovely, and when she is ready to return to Yorkshire, you will tell her that you are staying in London.'

'Sir. I have no wish to stay in London. I . . . ' But before I could say more, I was again roughly silenced by more passionate embraces. 'Listen Sophy. This house shall, be yours. I will have the deeds transferred to your name, only be kind to me. I am not an old man, Sophy . . . '

'But you are a drunken one, sir,' I retorted, trying to push him away. 'Have you no respect for me . . . or for Lady Perriman?'

Again the foolish, drunken laughter. 'Respect? Who wants respect? Not me. I want you, Sophy. Don't be afraid Sophy. I'll find you a rich husband . . . an accommodating husband . . . who'll close his eyes, when I tell him . . . close his eyes . . . '

His voice trailed away. Perhaps if I lay supine for a while, his hold on me might slacken. Then I could escape, but how or where, I had no notion. Idea after idea passed through my brain, when suddenly his Lordship gave a violent snore, at the same time loosening his embrace. He was actually asleep! Now was my chance. Gradually I edged myself from his arms and from off the sofa, and stood looking down at the man who, with his mouth wide open, presented a much less handsome personage than the elegant, handsome Lord Hugh Perriman.

I was still in a dangerous predicament. To whom could I go for help without causing a scandal? It would mean bitter distress for Aunt Lucy; and Mary and Barbara were such innocents. I could waken Martha, but hardly without rousing Dorcas, and she was such a gossip that she would relish spreading the story with her own embellishments. To fetch Lord Hugh's valet, or one of the household servants was equally dangerous; the incident might be commonplace to them and would occasion hearty laughter below stairs, but ruination to me, and misery to my beloved Aunt Lucy.

Then an idea slowly presented itself. It, too, was risky, but it seemed the only way. No-one would be breakfasting before noon. Why not let Lord Hugh sleep off his drunken stupor, and then in a few hours time, urge him to go to his own room? It would mean seeing that the coast was clear . . . putting a chair under the door knob to prevent anyone else coming in . . . and if his valet wondered as to his master's absence, he well knew of the certain ladies he had brought with him, and could only guess as to his nocturnal companion.

Making the door secure, I pondered as to my safest retreat. By now I was feeling cold, so greatly daring, I crept into bed, drawing the curtains around me . . . but not to sleep. It was more than I dare, and I should need all my wits about me within the next few hours.

Sitting there, the warmth gradually seeping through me, and my fears receding, I began to think about the future.

His Lordship was now my enemy. He would have nothing but spite and ill-will towards me, now that I had spurned him. Most probably he would insist that Aunt Lucy sent me about my business. I should never hear from George again. Where should I be in two years' time when he returned? Sobs rose in my throat, but I had to stifle them, lest I awoke Lord Hugh. Time went by, one heart-rending possibility chasing another. Perhaps I dozed, but suddenly I again heard movements. Daringly, I pulled a bed curtain aside. It was Lord Hugh cautiously moving the chair from beneath the door knob! Then, with equal caution, he opened the door, stepped outside, and almost noiselessly, closed the door behind him.

I could hardly believe it. The nightmare was over. Then the tears came . . . wonderful, relief giving tears. There would be no scandal, and I had emerged from the horror . . . unscathed . . . save for the fact that His Lordship would be a bitter antagonist to deal with.

★ ★ ★

I awoke with a start for the sun was streaming through the window, but looking at the little clock on the mantlepiece, I almost laughed with relief. It was only ten o'clock. I sat up in bed to review last night's happenings. Had it been real, or had it been a nightmare? To sleep again was impossible, so I decided to dress and go down to the breakfast room in search of a dish of tea.

Everywhere seemed deserted, except for servants cleaning the rooms, but on my entry, a footman was immediately at my side. I decided I felt hungry and within a few moments, I was partaking of bread and butter and tea.

What should I do next? Lady Perriman had forbidden that any of us went out alone, but I felt so restless and perturbed, that I knew not how to contain myself.

Then the breakfast room door was opened, and his Lordship walked over to the table, bowing courteously to me before seating himself in the chair held out by the footman.

' 'Twould seem, Miss Sophy, that we are the only two early risers.'

I felt gauche and awkward, and stammered some ridiculous reply. I had finished my breakfast, and longed to get up and run from the room, but for the life of me I seemed frozen to the chair. Lord Hugh, in the meantime, seemed to be enjoying his breakfast of thick gammon, kidneys and eggs, much to my surprise after his sorry condition last night.

I sipped at the remains of my tea, now grown cold. His Lordship noted my distaste and motioned to the hovering footman. 'Another cup of fresh tea for Miss Barton . . . and then you may go.'

I drew a long breath as I watched

the tea being poured, and finally the closing of the door. What was it that he had to say?

He looked so handsome, the perfect English gentleman, as he sat regarding me. Then. 'Miss Barton. Sophy. Last night I was the world's uttermost blackguard . . . I do not know how to apologise to you . . . '

'Perhaps, sir, it would be better if neither of us spoke of it again . . . '

'But I must have your forgiveness, Sophy. To plead that I was drunk, is no real excuse . . . '

'But that was the reason, sir . . . and I do forgive you . . . with all my heart. What is the saying, 'When the wine's in, the wit's out,' ' I babbled, so happy that the incident was to be closed.

He laughed ruefully. 'Generous as ever, little Sophy. That's how you've been towards all my family, ever since you came into the household. What few times I have been up in Yorkshire, I have noticed it. Why have you not yet married, Sophy?'

The suddenness of the question unnerved me. 'Why, sir . . . because . . . I suppose, because nobody has asked me,' I said foolishly.

' . . . and, that, because no-one is aware of the size of your dowry . . . '

'I have no dowry, sir.' My voice was low, almost ready to blurt out the story of my childhood.

'Who says you have no dowry? I shall make it widely known, that it is of a handsome size, worthy of such a beautiful bride . . . '

'But why, sir? Not as an apology . . . ?'

'Have I ever thanked you for saving my son's life?'

At the mention of George, I felt the colour leave my cheeks. Here was Lord Hugh prepared to give me a handsome dowry when I married . . . and I was already promised to his son.

Mercifully, His Lordship did not notice my consternation, for he went on, 'When you do marry, Sophy, I beg of you to be certain that you love the man and that he loves you.'

Again his earnestness, so contrary to his last night's flagrant behaviour, amazed me. How dare he talk of love, when he was so callous in his attitude towards his wife, flaunting his mistresses around London and Brighton?

'You have a great affection for Lady Perriman, have you not?'

'Indeed, sir. She has been like an angel from Heaven towards me.'

He rose from the table, noisily pushing back his chair, and strode over to the window, looking out in the street. Then with vehemence, ' . . . and she has been like an angel from Hell towards me.'

I, too, rose from my chair. 'Sir. I do not understand. I beg that you will excuse me.'

He came back to the table. 'Of course you do not understand. I, myself, do not understand. Sit down, Miss Sophy. Having gone so far, I claim the privilege of unburdening myself for the first time in my married life.'

I found myself obeying, sitting down, under the spell of his blazing, brown eyes.

'My marriage to Lucy Ashby was arranged by our parents. On my side there was a title . . . on hers . . . wealth. The Perriman estate needed money, but even so, with me, it was love at first sight. She was beautiful . . . gentle . . . as she is today. I was over the moon with joy. If she was not already in love with me, I would teach her to love me. Had she ever told you of those early days?'

'Never, sir. Never. She never discusses her personal affairs.'

He laughed bitterly and again walked over to the window, his back to me. 'There were never any to discuss. Right from the beginning, she made it clear to me, love was out of the question. Oh, yes, she was a dutiful, submissive wife . . . our brood of children proves that . . . but not one was conceived in love . . . only duty. Do these revelations disgust you, Miss Barton?'

I shook my head. 'Nothing about Lady Perriman could disgust me.'

'Bah! Loyalty! But Sophy, have you no compassion for me? Night after night, month after month, I tried to win her love, but there was never a flicker of response; not even the pressure of a hand . . . her heart is of stone, cold, hard, gritty stone.'

'But,' I floundered, 'she adores the children . . . everyone of them . . . '

'I know. I could almost hate them . . . that they should have the love denied to me . . . yet they owe their very existence to my love for her.'

'But there must be a reason, sir . . . '

'Why she doesn't love me? It's no use Sophy. No matter how many times I ask that question, there is no answer. The only conclusion I have come to, is that marriage without mutual love is as barren as if it were childless.'

'I am sorry, sir. Indeed I am . . . '

' . . . that is why I'm saying now, be sure that you love the man you marry and that he loves you. Never mind his wealth or position . . . ask yourself if you are prepared to make every sacrifice . . . to be poor, if fate so decrees. Now I've talked enough, Sophy, but thank you for listening. As to the dowry, have no fear of it being conscience money. It was one of the matters Lady Perriman and I discussed with the lawyers yesterday, before . . . '

'Thank you, sir.' My voice came as a whisper, but I managed a smile' . . . and I'll remember what you said about . . . '

He laughed as though he hadn't a care in the world . . . the incident behind him . . . forgotten . . . but I knew that the laughter was but a facade for his aching heart.

'Sensible young lady . . . and what's more, in the absence of any male relative, I'll give you away.'

As I dropped a curtsey, I lowered my eyes, lest he should see the sudden fear. He would never give me away to his son. Despite all his advice, he would want a lady of good birth and breeding for the next Lady Perriman.

★ ★ ★

We left London two days later, Lord Perriman having already returned to Brighton. We were all glad to be going home. I think we girls were all equally disillusioned, and Mary was beginning to miss her Henry. For my part, I felt physically sick with the rich wallowing in their overflow of luxury and the poor rotting in their hunger and squalor.

As we left the streets of London behind, Aunt Lucy lowered the carriage windows and with the first breath of country air, I felt impelled to voice my opinions.

'Why do the rich . . . who have plenty to spare, not help the poor?'

Aunt Lucy seemed lost for a reply. 'It is a matter of politics my dear . . . and politics are not the business of women folk . . . '

'Why not? Women can often see

further than men . . . can see the evil
. . . At the assembly the other night,
I heard murmurings of a possible
revolution . . . as they had in France . . . '

'Oh no, Sophy, no.' It was Barbara
who seemed really alarmed. 'You don't
think so, Mama, do you?'

'No, Barbara, no.' her mother soothed.
'We English are more restrained . . . '

'But those men, who band together
and march on London, are not
restrained. True, they use but sticks
and stones, but if once they get hold
of ammunition . . . '

'From where have you got all
this revolutionary talk?' laughed Lady
Perriman. 'They come but to ask for
more wages . . . more work . . . '

'Then why do they not get them?
Surely there are some politicians
. . . some wealthy landowners . . . some
wealthy manufacturers . . . who can
sympathise with them?'

'Sophy, you will have to marry a
politician and then you can sway him
to your way of thinking . . . '

'If he is not already to my way of thinking, I want none of him,' I countered, but now, on the question that was also uppermost in my mind, Barbara was again pestering her Mama.

'How do you know when you are in love, Mama?'

Her mother regarded her steadily. 'You had better ask Mary. She is the latest victim.'

Mary closed her eyes. 'Oh, it is something, no-one can explain. He is always in your mind. You are living for the moment when you will next be together . . . '

I closed my eyes and willed the presence of Julian Masters and there he was in the carriage beside me, my arm through his, smiling into each other's eyes. I switched my thoughts over to George but try as I would, he remained remote . . . far away. I closed my eyes tighter still, willing myself into his arms, longing to savour again those rapturous kisses but all I could conjure up was the boy . . . always my admirer, my champion, 'Let Sophy decide' . . . perpetually seeking my advice in all our childish exploits, delegating me as leader. To be the dominating partner in marriage would be most distasteful. I wanted a man to whom I could turn in times of stress . . . a man who could be master of his fate . . . and mine. Was George that man . . . or Julian.

4

All was hustle and bustle at Perriman Court for Mary was to be married early in December. New carpets, drapes and furniture were arriving daily for there had been no big family gathering at the Court for many years and Lord Hugh had given orders that no expense was to be spared. His mother, the Dowager Lady Perriman, now an old lady, was to be one of the principal guests together with her three daughters and their husbands, each bringing several sons and daughters of varying ages.

Daily, Martha issued stern warnings to the children and servants alike that they would have to watch their behaviour as strong, carping criticism could be expected from that quarter. When I asked about guests from Aunt Lucy's family, Martha looked grim.

'There'll be none of them coming,

God be thanked.' This was a statement, inquisitive Barbara could not let pass. 'Why not Nannie?'

'Because there's none of them left . . . least not in this country . . . '

'Then where are they all?'

'Her Ladyship's parents are dead and her brother and his wife are away in the Indies.' There was a pause and then in a low mutter, ' . . . and that's where they want to stay . . . '

'Why?'

'You ask too many questions, Miss Barbara. There will be plenty of Perriman cousins to be entertained, not to mention all the friends your Papa has invited . . . and a word of warning . . . don't tell your Mama that you've been asking questions about her family.'

'Really, Nannie, I don't understand. Surely we should be informed about our Aunt and Uncle. Is it that there's a scandal attached to them? Did they elope? Do tell us, Nannie.'

'They did not elope, and I've told you

too much already. It doesn't concern you in any way, so ask no more questions, Miss.'

Yet I, too, was vastly intrigued about Uncle Martyn. I had never heard his name mentioned before. As Barbara suggested, there must be some dreadful secret connected with him.

* * *

As the wedding-day drew nearer, so Aunt Lucy seemed to rely more on me; to take me more into her confidence. When I had thanked her for arranging to give me a dowry, she had tried to pass off the subject, merely remarking that although it had been in her mind for sometime, it was Lord Hugh who had put the matter into his lawyer's hands.

To my surprise, when I remarked on his kindness and generosity, she had burst into tears.

Nonplussed, I asked, 'Dear Aunt Lucy. What is wrong?'

'Nothing, child, nothing. Like you, I was overwhelmed at his Lordship's generosity. I had not thought that he cared aught about you. His action took me completely unawares, but it made me so happy . . . so very happy . . . and then . . . '

She dabbed her eyes. 'It was the night of the assembly; do you remember? Everything was going so well . . . at least at the beginning of the evening . . . then with the drinking . . . everyone seemed to go wild . . . and I came across Lord Hugh kissing some odious creature!'

'Oh no, Aunt Lucy. You were jealous?'

'Jealous? I don't know. I was angry. To think that he could so behave . . . when his wife and daughters were present . . . He tried to laugh it off . . . said it was time I came out of my Yorkshire Convent . . . I answered him like a vixen . . . and that creature laughed, and went off no doubt to tell the others . . . and Lord Hugh became more furious than ever. That night, I bolted my door against him . . . and ever since . . . I have been so ashamed . . . oh so very ashamed.'

So that was the explanation. Already too full of drink; spurned by his wife; inflamed by still more drink taken to drown his humiliation, his befuddled brain had directed him to my room.

In that moment, my loyalty wavered; I did not know for whom I had the greater sympathy.

'Perhaps when he comes up for the wedding . . . '

'I hope so. I sent him a note of apology . . . but he has not answered . . . but then, neither of us have ever been good letter writers.'

★ ★ ★

Tomorrow was Mary's wedding day. Already the house was filling up with guests, Lord Hugh having arrived two days ago, and amazing us all by saying that he was considering staying over Christmas, and still to my greater astonishment . . . and satisfaction . . . Aunt Lucy seemingly pleased at the prospect.

For the first wedding in the family, Lady Perriman had decided that it should be an all Yorkshire affair, everything for the wedding-breakfast being produced on the estate, be it the carcasses of beef, mutton or pork; the huge, succulent Yorkshire hams, or the tasty, meaty capons. Hundreds of jars of bottled fruit had been brought out from the preserve cupboards, and night after night for the past few weeks, gardeners had stayed up, so that an even heat could be maintained in the hot houses, where myriads of blooms were waiting to be brought out for decoration.

Down in the kitchens, whole carcasses were being roasted on the huge spits, and from the ovens, perspiring bakers were drawing out batch after batch of all manner of pies and tarts. In the confectioner's room, his assistants were frantically whipping bowls of cream and egg whites by means of little besoms composed of birch twigs, while he, himself, was occupied in icing cakes and gateaux with the aid of a tiny feather brush.

Priceless silver and gold plate had been taken from vaults, all to be cleaned and polished along with hundreds of pieces of beautiful cut glass.

I had been taught to love everything beautiful, so that I was no Philistine, but why, I wondered, was it necessary to make such ornate show on the occasion of uniting two people in marriage? Why all the gluttonous eating and drinking?

★ ★ ★

I was still pondering on this question, when, dressed in my gown of white silk, festooned with tiers of lace, I stood behind Mary and her bridegroom, listening to our own dear chaplain, the Rev. Mr. Long intoning the service.

With its profusion of massed blooms,

the chapel had never seemed so beautiful, and the bitter-sweet scent of the chrysanthemums mixed with the heavy perfume of forced spring flowers, pervaded the air.

I had been a guest at several weddings, but never before had I really heeded the words of the service. Now, I listened intently, and found beauty in them. Perhaps, I reasoned, all this display of fine clothes, jewels and hot house flowers were essential as a background, to emphasise the importance of the occasion; the mixture of solemnity and joy. I looked at Mary and Henry. Their faces radiated happiness. I looked at Aunt Lucy and Lord Hugh; he the picture of equanimity; she serene and smiling. Why had Aunt Lucy gone into marriage, knowing that she did not love him? Had she been so much under her parents' domination? Now as I glanced up at them again, I had the oddest feeling, that a change was coming . . . a mellowing and a better understanding.

Mr. Long gave but a short sermon; emphasising love and duty towards each other. Throughout, I noticed Lord and Lady Perriman kept their eyes downcast. Dear Mr. Long, he must have been well aware of the position, for he was a valuable and trusted friend, and being childless, both he and Mrs. Long adored the Perriman children, Mr. Long becoming our tutor as each passed the governess age.

Then it was all over. The village church bells could be heard pealing out their joyous message and the feasting and drinking began to get well under way, tables having been set up both in the big banqueting hall and in the gallery. Being at the top table, I noticed with delight that Aunt Lucy and Lord Hugh were apparently in excellent spirits, talking animatedly, but what gave me greater joy, was to notice that Lord Hugh was drinking but sparingly.

The young Perrimans, free of all restrictions for this wondrous occasion were having high jinks; even Charles being brought in to be passed from Mama to Papa and to Grandmother; a picture of truly happy, family life. Please God, I prayed, let it last. Two such kind people deserve happiness.

★ ★ ★

The newly-weds spent their wedding night at Perriman Court, leaving early the next morning on the first stage of their honeymoon . . . a tour of the Continent.

As I waved them goodbye, I was recalling Mary's words as she had kissed me. 'You next, Sophy. There's quite a few of my cousins already partial to you. They, themselves, have told me.'

I had laughed in reply, not daring to tell her of my promise to George . . . a promise I now rued . . . not because I had ceased to love him any less, but because I was daily becoming more and more confused about this question of love and marriage.

Now Aunt Lucy was busy arranging entertainments for her guests who were staying on for three or four days, and seeking my assistance.

'They're all saying you next,' muttered Martha, 'but what her Ladyship will do then I just don't know.'

'Well, that won't be for a long time,' I began.

'You never know, Miss Sophy . . . and if you can find a good man . . . take him . . . that's what I say.'

I felt a rising compassion for the kindly old woman who had done so much for me . . . who knew so much about me.

'Why have you never married, Martha?'

She turned away her head, but I saw the corner of the snow-white apron being lifted up to her eye and her voice was husky as she answered.

'That's an old, old story, Miss Sophy. There was a man . . . he was a footman and I was an under-nursemaid. We were to have been married, as soon as there was an empty lodge for us . . . then one night when he was down in the village . . . the press-gang came . . . '

I was quick to put my arm around her as her voice faltered. 'I never saw him again. They say he fought and resisted . . . the master was away at the time or he might have done something . . . '

'Poor, dear Martha . . . '

'I waited several years . . . hoping . . . then the children grew up and I looked for a new place, and so became nurse to her Ladyship . . . '

'And you've been with her ever since . . . ever since she was a baby?'

'Yes. To me she has been my baby. I watched her grow up . . . I saw . . . I knew . . . all about her . . . then . . . then . . . ' She suddenly stopped and pulled herself together, with an attempt at briskness in her speech . . . 'Well then, she got married . . . and I came with her as her personal maid.'

'Thank you for telling me, Martha. I always knew there was a strong bond between you.'

'Well, don't you go talking to her Ladyship about these matters ... I must have had too much of that fancy wine or I shouldn't have spoken so freely ...'

Why didn't Aunt Lucy wish to talk of the past? Again the feeling of some grim, dark secret.

We had just finished arranging the tables in the card room, when Lord Hugh came breezing in, searching for Aunt Lucy.

'She was in the dining-room, sir, supervising the arrangement of the flowers,' I volunteered.

'Thank you, Miss Sophy. I'll find her. In the meantime, go get yourself a warm cloak, and see that the children are well wrapped. Then bring them down to the stables. By way of a diversion, we're arranging a parade and a drive through the nearby villages ... just for about an hour ... to work up an appetite for lunch.'

Martha looked at me with a grimace. 'Orders are orders, Miss Sophy. Better go and get the children ready.'

As I passed the dining-room, I could hear Lord Hugh's voice. 'Come on, Lucy. It will do you good to get a breath of fresh air . . . and I'd rather have you beside me than any other woman here . . .'

Would she accompany him, I wondered, as I went up to the nursery. The children needed no second bidding, delighted to get out of the schoolroom, and warmly wrapped, we all trooped off to the stables, Charles staggering along, holding my hand.

Every piece of equipage had been brought out; carriages, tilburys, phaetons, dog-carts; some belonging to the guests, some being put at the disposal of anyone wishing to drive. The horses, after their two or three days' rest, save for yard exercise, were pawing the ground impatiently, anxious to be away, their coats glistening with good grooming, their harness bright and immaculate with much elbow-grease.

I was holding Charles in my arms, so that he could get a good view of all that was going on, and it was he who espied them first. 'Mama! Papa!' he called, pointing in their direction. So Aunt Lucy was joining him!

They did indeed look a handsome pair. He, tall and robust in his faultlessly cut dark blue riding clothes; and she in a warm, loose cloak, and on her head a black velour hat, trimmed with several royal blue ostrich feathers, and tied under her chin with a large bow of matching blue tuelle.

They came over to us, and Lord Hugh, lifting Charles from me, took him to see the horses, followed by the little girls. Barbara and I remaining with Aunt Lucy.

What a pandemonium! Whinnying horses; men's loud laughter; women's tinkling and giggling mixed with the crunch of wheels, as vehicles moved out of the cobbled yard into the long drive. Now Lord Hugh was back with the children.

'Come Lucy, we're giving our new tilbury an airing . . . '

'Charles wants to come,' came a small protest.

'No, my darling. You stay with Sophy. She'll look after you.' His mother kissed him and put him back in my arms. Then Caroline, Sara and Elizabeth stepped forward to be kissed. Charles crowed with delight. 'Kiss Ba-Ba . . . and Sophy.' Aunt Lucy complied. 'Now Papa . . . kiss everybody.'

'Nothing would please me better, my son,' was his father's laughing response, as he gallantly kissed us all, before taking Aunt Lucy by the hand, and leading her to the tilbury.

'Do you not think, Sophy, that they seem very happy these days?' asked Barbara.

'I do indeed. It must be wedding fever. Everybody seems intoxicated with it . . . '

'All except me,' bewailed Barbara, ' . . . and there's not one man here that I feel partial towards.'

'Nor me. So we'll grow into old maids together,' I laughed.

'But I don't want to be an old maid . . . '

'Don't pester yourself. You won't. Oh look, Lord Hugh and Aunt Lucy are up in their tilbury! Can you see them, Sara? Caroline? Elizabeth? Wave to them as they go by!'

Everybody was jostling everybody else, in an effort to get themselves into some semblance of order. There were several horse-riders, both ladies and gentlemen, and they were to lead off. At last the procession was moving to the cheers and hurrahs of the on-lookers, including stable-boys and yard-men, who had had a hard morning's work and were glad to see them go, to get a short respite.

As she passed, Aunt Lucy waved and threw kisses but Lord Hugh was too busy with his reins. We watched until the last carriage was out of sight, and then made our way back to the house, where Martha, dear thoughtful Martha, had cups of hot chocolate awaiting us.

* * *

Now the children were pestering that we should go out again to see the return of the horses and carriages, and I was finding it hard work to restrain their impatience.

'Just a few minutes longer, before we go out into the cold air again,' I protested.

I was fastening Charles' coat when we heard footsteps racing along the nursery landing, and a footman, without bothering to knock, burst in. 'Miss Sophia. Miss Barbara. There's a messenger downstairs . . . come quick . . . there's been an accident.'

Bidding a nurse take charge of the children, we ran downstairs. Would we never reach the hall below? Never before had the staircase seemed so long, but at last we were being allowed to pass through the silent groups of guests and servants, towards the gentlemen I now recognised as having been at the head of the parade, and now came to meet us.

'I've raced ahead young ladies, to prepare you . . . '

'For what, sir? What has happened?'

Barbara and I almost shouted the question, and it was Martha, hobbling towards us, who moaned, 'He's killed her. He's killed her!'

'What are you saying, Martha? How do you know?' I turned to the gentleman, but he had moved over to the window from where, two closed carriages could be seen being gently led along the drive. Other vehicles were following, but nowhere could I see the smart Perriman tilbury.

For a moment, I knew panic. I thought I would swoon. In the background, I could hear Barbara screaming . . . Martha attempted to quieten her. Then someone called,

'Two trestle tops for stretchers.'

'Two? Did that mean two people were hurt? God, oh God, why didn't Aunt Lucy and Lord Hugh show themselves? Now I could discern Barbara's screams. 'It's Mama and Papa! I know it is.'

It was Aunt Lucy they were now lifting from the carriage. I could tell by the bright blaze of blue feathers hanging down her cloak, her hat having fallen backwards, still tied under her chin.

Unable to move, I watched them place her on a trestle, with cushions under her head and a carriage rug thrown over her. Then, carefully, she was carried up the big stone stairway into the hall, and then through into the library. Barbara and Martha were still clinging together, but suddenly, my legs were galvanised into action, and I dashed into the room where Aunt Lucy, still on the trestle, lay on the floor.

Her eyes were closed. There was a

big, ugly bruise on her left temple, but otherwise seemed uninjured. As I took her hand, I was shocked to feel how cold it was, and instinctively put it under the rug.

'The doctor should be here any moment, Miss Barton. A rider went for him straightaway.'

'Wouldn't she be more comfortable if she was on a sofa?' I asked chokingly.

'Better not move her until the doctor has seen her. We think she has broken her . . . '

At this moment, there was a flicker of her eyelids, and Lucy Perriman gazed up at me. A smile radiated her face as she whispered. 'Sophy. My very own little Sophy.' She put out her hand and I took it and held it to my lips, the tears running down my cheeks.

I was then aware that Martha was on the ground beside me calling frantically, 'Miss Lucy. Miss Lucy.' With her hand still in mine, Lady Perriman moved her head restlessly, 'It's Martha, isn't it? Look after her for me, Martha.' She gave a tired little sigh, and someone behind me spoke. 'Here comes the doctor.'

I rose to my feet and watched as he began his examination. He seemed almost frightened and looked around with an air of disbelief, then without a word, he drew the blanket over the lovely face of Lucy Perriman.

* * *

I hadn't noticed anything else going on in the room, but as someone came and put a comforting arm around me, to lead me out, I came to a stunned standstill as I noticed another group round another, rug-draped trestle.

I felt every bit of life being drained from me. It must be Lord Hugh, and he was dead. Were people actually screaming and shouting and sobbing, or was it all in the uproarious clanging of my brain?

Mercifully I slid into unconciousness, but even so, again I heard Lady

Perriman's voice. 'My little Sophy. My very own little Sophy.'

When I awoke, I was in bed, in my night-clothes. A fire burned brightly in the grate and for a brief moment I felt wonderfully at ease. Then memory came flooding back. I pulled the bell violently and when Dorcas came, I demanded, 'What is the time? Why am I in bed?'

' 'Tis six o'clock, Miss Sophia . . . and you are in bed under the doctor's orders. He gave you an opiate . . . '

'And the other ladies?'

'All sleeping off their opiates . . . '

'But the children?'

'They're safe and sound up in the nursery. The Rev. and Mrs. Long came and took charge.'

I gave a sigh of relief. 'Miss Barbara?'

'She's taken it very bad . . . so she got a special heavy dose . . . '

'And the Dowager Lady . . . '

'Hard as a rock. Her lady daughters drooping all around her, but she's bearing up.'

'And I'm getting up, Dorcas. I can't stay here in bed just thinking . . . ' My voice was choked, but I fought back the tears. Those children upstairs needed me. Then I suddenly remembered Martha.

'Oh, she's been given a heavy opiate too. In a very bad way she is, but then she's old . . . '

'Old or not, she was devoted to her Ladyship. I must go and see her.'

As I gazed down on Martha, breathing heavily, I echoed Dorcas' words. She was old . . . and lying there, immobile, she looked like some venerable old nun.

I did not dare venture downstairs to meet the Perriman family . . . I dare not intrude on their grief . . . much as I would have appreciated the sharing of it. When they sent for Barbara and her sisters, I knew they intended to ignore me. I was not even asked to take meals with them, and while the insult hurt, I was relieved to be able to stay in the nursery with Charles, for he was my only source of comfort; Martha being almost in a state of collapse and keeping to her bed.

Gradually, mostly from Barbara, Dorcas and Mr. Long, I pieced together the story of the tragedy. No-one had been indulging in mad driving, but the tilbury, being a light-weight vehicle, was able to reach the highest speed. Lord Hugh had it under perfect control, until some small animal . . . a stoat or a weasel, ran out from the hedgerow, right under the horse's hooves. The horse reared, then dashed away. The wheel of the tilbury became fixed in a frozen rut, and as the horse pulled, so the tilbury went over, throwing its two passengers. No-one was sure whether their injuries were due to the hard, frozen road, or whether the horses kicked them. Help was to hand almost immediately, but it was obvious both were seriously hurt. As they lay on the rime-frosted grass verge, Lady Lucy had been heard to say, 'I'm so sorry Hugh . . . so very sorry.' Lord

Hugh had reached out for her hand, and as their fingers touched, his last words were, 'I love you, Lucy. I've always loved you.' He was dead when they lifted him into the carriage.

5

Without any loss of time, a courier had been sent in pursuit of the newlyweds to prevent them crossing over to the Continent. Poor little bride. How terrible to have her happiness shattered in such a manner but how grateful she should be to have the strength of a loving husband beside her. Fortunately, they had got no further than London.

Another courier, with instructions to travel overland wherever practicable, in order to reach George as quickly as possible, had been despatched to India bearing news of the tragedy and his succession to the title. It was Mr. Long, who informed me that representations were being made in the proper places to get the new Lord Perriman released from his military duties so as to return home to take over the care of his young brothers and sisters and his large estate.

The realisation took away my breath. George would be home in a matter of months . . . not years . . . and I was his betrothed wife! How would those aristocratic Perrimans, sitting in the darkened rooms, react, if I was to make the announcement? Since the tragedy, I had partaken all my meals in the nursery with the children, for while Barbara and twelve year-old Caroline were invited to join their grandmother and other relatives, I was left out. At first, I didn't mind. I had no wish to eat . . . or talk . . . but as the dreadful days passed on slowly, the fact that I was practically banished from the family life, gave me much time to think and brood.

What plans were they making for the care of the children? What would happen to me? Sometimes in my misery, I would long for George's presence, telling myself that to marry him would be the solution of all my problems; a wondrous, glorious solution . . . to be Lady Perriman. Then I would recall Lord Hugh's warning, not to marry without love, and my misery would become even greater, for now, save for old Martha, I had no-one's affection.

★ ★ ★

The chapel bell had been tolling since noon. Another two hours before the funeral service! I felt I could bear it no longer. No invitation had come for me to join the family mourners; to them I was but an unpaid servant. Martha was still in a state of near collapse, and on the doctor's advice and my cajolery, she had been persuaded to stay with Charles and the two youngest girls, but I felt that I must attend, to say farewell to my beloved adopted Aunt Lucy, no matter how humble my placing.

Throwing on a cloak, I slipped down the stairs and out of a side door. Which direction should I take? To the lakeside where George and I had made our vows, or towards the plantations where it would be more sheltered from the biting wind?

I walked blindly . . . aimlessly along the drive of tall trees, their naked branches looking stark and ghoulish in the grey of the afternoon. The woods looked dark and forbidding. How often we had played in there . . . knowing nothing of fear . . . revelling in the beauty of it all. I left the drive and walked over to the open parkland stumbling over gnarled roots.

Suddenly I could go no further. All my pent-up anguish threatened me with nausea. I almost collapsed on to a fallen tree — the site of so many of our imaginative games. I put my head down and lying there, sobbed out my misery.

I don't know whether I went into a swoon or that having drained the depth of my grief I found ease and quietude, but gradually I became aware that someone was kneeling beside me with an arm around my shoulder. As I turned the man spoke.

'Miss Sophia? Are you all right?'

It was Julian Masters. My heart leapt with sudden thankfulness. I had an urge to tell him how glad I was to see him; how much I needed him, but my bewildered brain could not put my thoughts into words.

With his arm still around me and sensing my inadequacy, he went on, 'I saw you stumble over here . . . your distress . . . '

'How long have you been here?'

'Long enough to know that you are suffering deeply . . . '

'You . . . you had no right to trespass on . . . on my personal feelings . . . '

'No? Here take my handkerchief. Your eyes are still full of tears.' He took from my hand the little screwed up ball of wet cambric. 'This trifle is of small use.' He watched me for a moment. 'May I express my deepest sympathy for you all. The two young ladies?'

'Miss Mary was married the day before . . . before it happened. Miss

Barbara is bearing up bravely.'

'Ah . . . A Perriman shows no fear. Isn't that the family motto?'

'Then it is obvious that I am lacking in the Perriman virtues for you find here a veritable cry-baby. You, Sir, I take it have come . . . ' Again tears threatened my composure.

'To pay my last respects . . . yes. I told you when we last met, that though of short acquaintance, I was deeply attached to his lordship. As for you, Miss Sophia, I find you no cry-baby, but of extra compassionate nature.'

I looked at him and a stupid little laugh escaped me. 'That shows how little you can estimate my feelings, Sir, for at this moment, I am full of anger . . . full of bitterness . . . I feel I loathe and despise everyone. Now can you understand what an undesirable person I am?'

By now we were both sitting upright on the tree trunk and I was amazed to find my voice so well under control and to see the flicker of a smile cross Mr. Master's face.

'That's better, Miss Sophia. Like to tell me what has made you so angry?'

' 'Tis a family affair,' I began primly. Then I stopped. The Perrimans had made it clear that I was not one of the family.

'To begin with . . . I have not been asked to join the family mourning party . . . secondly . . . I have not yet been told of any arrangements being made for the children . . . nor what they wish me to do . . . '

I don't know when he had taken my hand between his, but I let it remain there. His well-kept hands were warm and alive — they made me feel wanted . . . they gave me strength.

'Does it really matter whether, when you say farewell and that last little prayer, does it matter with whom you stand . . . dowager, duchess, or scullery-maid?' His voice was low and soothing. 'As for the future . . . whatever happens . . . whatever

they say to you . . . stand up to them
. . . say what you wish to say . . . don't
be afraid . . . '

'It is for the children, I'm afraid. Not
knowing . . . They're so accustomed to
being loved and cherished . . . now
. . . they have no-one . . . If I am sent
away.'

'Pray God that doesn't happen. It
won't happen if they have any sense.'
The bell ceased tolling. I got to my
feet quickly. 'They are gathering in the
chapel . . . I must go.'

'Will you allow me to stand with
you, Miss Sophia?'

I did not hesitate. 'Thank you, Sir
. . . I should be grateful . . . '

We were almost running along the
drive, with no breath for talking. Along
with several of the Perriman staff, we
squeezed into a back pew, and silently
knelt in prayer.

I rose to my feet as Mr. Long began
to read the service, but, being almost
unable to control his emotion, I could
barely discern the words. Only a week

ago since he was reading the marriage service . . . everyone happy . . . happier than they had been for years. Were Lord Hugh and Aunt Lucy really happy now? Had all misunderstandings been washed away?

The bell was again tolling. Estate workers were taking up their positions to shoulder the mortal remains of their late master and mistress; to take them on their last journey to the family vault.

As the flower-covered coffins approached our pew, the sobs in my throat refused to be held back and unashamedly I stood there and let the tears course down my cheeks at the same time finding such comfort in Julian Masters' firm handgrip. When everyone else had gone, I knelt down once again and prayed . . . prayed for guidance.

We were the last out of the chapel and found ourselves alone; the gentlemen having gone on to the vault; the ladies to the comfort of their rooms and the servants to their tasks. Now my heart cried out against the imminent parting from Mr. Masters, but from someone, or from somewhere, a calm comfort had descended upon me so that I was able to hold out my hand, saying.

'I am indeed grateful for your company, sir. You will never know what it meant to me.'

'Perhaps, some day, you will tell me Miss Sophia. I shall be coming north again in about a month's time. May I call on you?'

So it wasn't goodbye! But where would I be in a month's time?

'I doubt if I shall be here, Sir. I know nothing of my future movements . . . '

'Then your address, that I might call on you, elsewhere . . . '

I shook my head. 'I have no address, sir.'

'Then there's only one thing for it.' From his waistcoat pocket he took out a case, extracted a card and handed it to me.

'My London address and if you

leave Perriman Court, will you promise to write and let me know your whereabouts?'

For a second, I hesitated. Such indelicate behaviour was all so foreign to Aunt Lucy's teaching, yet to who else could I turn, if need be?

I nodded, too overcome to speak. He took my hand. 'You're cold, Miss Sophia. Run along, indoors ... and God be with you.' Gently he lifted my hand and kissed it, then turning on his heel, quickly strode away.

For a brief moment I watched him, then hastened into the house. As I entered the warm, cosy nursery, Martha looked up.

'We are both to go down to the library for the reading of the wills ... after dinner.'

★ ★ ★

The family was already gathered, when, with Martha on my arm, I entered the library. They stared at us with indifference, but Mr. Stevens, the attorney, indicated that chairs were to be brought for us. The servants who had followed us, took their stand along the wall as Mr. Stevens began to clear his throat.

'I regret that owing to certain circumstances the will of the late Lord Perriman will not be read on this occasion. but in accordance with the wishes of senior members of the family, the reading shall be postponed until the return of Lord George Perriman. However, in regard to her late ladyship's will, I can proceed.'

There were surprised exclamations and mutterings and it was some minutes before Mr. Stevens could continue.

It was a very simply worded will. There was a legacy for each member of her staff, according to length of service, the largest of all for Martha. I patted her hand comfortingly as I saw the tears rolling down her withered cheeks. Then I heard my name.

'To my dear ward, Sophia Barton, for all the love and joy she has given me . . . '

My head was in a whirl as a babble of talk burst out, only to be quietened by Mr. Stevens, as he continued the reading. The rest of her estate was to be shared between her children.

I hadn't fully comprehended the amount of my legacy but I had realised that it was sufficiently large to enable me to live in comfort and luxury.

Again Mr. Stevens called for silence to state that the family wished Miss Barton to remain, along with the members of the family. Slowly the servants filed out, elated at the prospect of money coming to them.

What was it they wanted of me?

Mr. Stevens was still the spokesman. 'On behalf of the family, I have been asked to draw up a statement as to the immediate future of the late Lord Perriman's family.

'Sir Henry and Lady Stainton are

prepared to give Miss Barbara a home with them, until her brother, Lord Perriman, returns home.' The late Lord Perriman's three sisters — here Mr. Stevens read out their names and titles and places of residence — were each prepared to take one daughter, until such time as their brother returned home, while the Dowager Lady Perriman would take baby Charles. It had been her intention to ask me to go as nurse, but in view of the fact that I was now of independant means, I would perhaps like to state my views.

I would indeed like to state my views. I was seething with dismay. How could they, I demanded, break up the family in such a callous way? Those children, now deprived of the mother they adored, were dependent on each other for mutual comfort. If only they had taken the trouble to visit the nursery this last week, they would have seen such heart-breaking grief; such lovable efforts to comfort one another, that they would never have contemplated separating them.

I heard angry dissension, especially among the ladies; but I didn't care. What was it Julian Masters had said? 'Stand up to them. Say what you wish to say.'

I looked from one to another of them, all looking so self-satisfied with their offer. 'Could not one of you take all four children?' There were snorts of indignation. 'How dare you! A young chit of no standing or position, telling us what to do!'

'I am not telling, ma'am . . . I am only suggesting.' A whole babble of dissension seemed to break out, punctuated every now and then by a man's guffaw of laughter.

At last, the banging of Grandmother Perriman's stick, caused the riot to subside, and she managed to make herself heard. 'There's something in what the girl says. Which of you will take them — all four?'

Again the gibble-gabble, now angry.

Again the banging of the stick. 'You see, girl. None of them will have your notion, so . . .'

'Stand up to them'. Julian was holding my hand, giving me strength. I'll swear I could feel the warmth.

'I think I know of someone who would take them all . . . someone of whom Lord and Lady Perriman would have approved . . .'

'And who might that be?' There was sarcasm in the well-bred voice.

I hesitated for a moment. What right had I to put the burden on other shoulders . . . but there I was blurting it out, 'The Rev. and Mrs. Long.'

For a moment there was silence, but her Ladyship was quick to demand, 'And what does the Rev. and Mrs. Long think of that idea?'

I waited with baited breath. Then the reverend gentleman was speaking, his voice full of poignancy.

'There's nothing that either my wife or myself would welcome more . . . a small way of repaying all the kindness that has been shown to us since we came to *Perriman Court*, many years ago.' He paused ' . . . there is one condition, however.'

'Yes?' It was almost a growl from grandmother.

' . . . that Miss Barton stays on . . . enjoying the same position as she has always had . . . '

That was the signal for another outburst. There were more angry epithets that I couldn't help over-hearing. 'She's not a fit person!' 'Who is she anyway?' 'La, my dear, you're jealous.' ' . . . and you're taken in by a pretty face.'

Martha and I continued to sit there, not knowing whether to leave in disgust, or to remain in dignity. At last Mr. Stevens came over to us. 'We are to discuss the matter again, and will let you know our decision in the morning.' I thanked him politely and was helping Martha to rise, when he whispered, 'The old lady is much taken up with your idea . . . and I'll encourage her!' I smiled my thanks, as I saw several other gentlemen smiling in my direction.

That night, when I went to sleep, I clasped in my hand a man's handkerchief, bearing the initial 'J' and as I lay there, willing sleep to come. I was again sitting on the tree-trunk, his arm around me. His gentleness and sympathy had brought about such a nearness. When would I see him again? I thought of George, now Lord Perriman. I could not marry him. The family would expect him to marry an heiress . . . the daughter of a titled family . . . not a workhouse brat!

* * *

It was wonderful. The Perriman stronghold had capitulated, Mr. and Mrs. Long and I were in charge of the children until George came home and the estate was to continue being run under the watchful eye of Mr. Storey the agent. I hugged Charles with joy. All would be well. George would return and find his family awaiting him.

When I told Martha, she had just looked at me in a dazed manner as though she could scarcely believe it.

'So you see, dear Martha, you must get well again. I need your help . . . your advice . . . and you.'

For the first time since the accident, she smiled; a wan, sad little smile.

'Yes, Miss Sophy, yes. Just till Master George comes home . . . no longer . . . then I'm ready to join her . . . just long enough to see you and Master George settled and happy . . . '

I looked at her keenly. Did she know anything? Or was she guessing? Or wishful thinking? Or was it my imagination?

6

'God rest you merry gentlemen,
Let nothing you dismay . . . '

'Let nothing you dismay,' I looked across at Barbara who had buried her head in a cushion and was sobbing noisily. Outside on the terrace, the carol-singers were lustily going through their repertoire, knowing that when finished, they would all come trooping in to hot toddy and mincepies as I had known them to do each Christmas Eve since I had come to Perriman Court. The joyousness of the carols only served to intensify our misery.

We had decided not to make any changes in our Christmas programmes . . . even the servants and estate workers' ball was to be held.

Looking back, I am sure it was the little ones who kept us from breaking down and even they sometimes would suddenly demand Mama and when they couldn't go to her, would weep tempestuously or go into a fit of tantrums.

It was heartbreaking to bring out those toys we had bought in London . . . to see the temporary pleasure on their faces but the pretty gowns and satin slippers had to remain in their wrappings, not to be worn until the period of mourning was over. Each time I saw those little girls in their ugly black dresses, I wanted to tear them from off their backs, longing to explode that angels in Heaven, didn't wear black!

Martha was no help. She went around muttering to herself but without any real conversation. 'Just till Master George gets back. That's all I ask' was the most I could get out of her.

The Perrimans had lost no time in leaving. They were anxious to get home before Christmas and I doubt whether the tragedy made much difference to their celebrations.

Somehow, we endured the agony of Christmas. The New Year was ushered in and I began to hope.

Julian Masters had said that he would be coming North in January and that he could call on me. How long would I have to wait? Again and again, he would intrude on my innermost thoughts. Again and again, I asked myself, what did this man mean to me . . . and I to him? Was he dearer to me than George . . . Could it be that I was in love with him? Or George, who now that he was a lord, I dare not marry.

Then came the snow, covering the whole of the countryside to such a depth as to make travel impossible. Estate-workers frantically dug roadways down to the village where we knew there were many with only a small stock of food and fuel. Together with Mr. and Mrs. Long, Barbara and I visited the sick and the poor. Except for the hardship some were suffering, I was glad of the diversion; something to engage our bruised minds.

It was the hardest winter I can remember. After the snow came the big freeze and it seemed those banks and drifts of frozen snow would never melt so that when the news filtered through that the same conditions prevailed over the whole country, I knew I would not be seeing Mr. Masters for some time to come.

Yet surprisingly, the knowledge did not dismay me; rather I felt that it was good that he was being kept away, feeling that the bond between us was being strengthened.

There was another unlooked-for benefit. The children revelled in the snow, and I joined in snow-fights and the making of a veritable army of snowmen; the exercise and cold air bringing back our dulled appetites, and more peaceful sleep at night.

It was towards the end of January that George's first letter arrived; not from India, but from some port en route, where mail had been collected. There was one for Lady Perriman, but Mr. Long decided, that in the absence of Mary, Barbara should open it and read it to her sisters.

They were just ordinary family letters, mine somewhat less restrained than the one written to his mother; both full of agonising detail about the terrible time in the Bay of Biscay; but full of enthusiasm about the strange sights where he had gone ashore. I searched for a snippet of paper, bearing a special message for me, but there was none, although he did sign himself, 'Your ever loving Geroge'. I had no compunction whatever about letting the rest of the family read it, feeling guilty that it gave me no elation . . . no lifting of my spirits.

January, February slowly dragged through their apportioned days. Surely March, which heralds the Spring, would see a change. It did indeed, for with the melting of the snow came the floods; floods that again imperilled all hope of safe travel.

With the days beginning to lengthen, some of our heaviness seemed to lift; the raw bleeding wounds were beginning to heal.

Since Christmas, we had been without a governess; Mamselle declaring that she must go home to her sick mother but in actuality we knew that being of a highly emotional nature, she could not stand the strained atmosphere at Perriman. Mr. Long and I had taken over the lessons only too glad to occupy our minds but we had now decided that we must obtain a governess who could give full time teaching to the girls.

Then came our first letters from India sent by overland mail. Seemingly, life in India was a riot of balls and dinners, according to George's brief epistle. My heart ached for him knowing that by now he must have received the news of the deaths of his parents. How soon would it be before he was back home? Mr. Long insisted that top priority having been given to his release he would most probably arrive in person . . . without warning. He assured us there was no point in answering these letters. He would be on his way home before they arrived. For this, I was truly thankful. It put off the moment when I would have to tell him that I could not marry him.

★ ★ ★

There were whoops of joy when I took the children to the stables to arrange the renewal of their riding lessons, Charles included. Mr. Long and our doctor had been most insistent that we should not give up riding or show fear of horses; far better to be brave and win back our confidence.

Going round the horse boxes with a plentiful supply of sugar lumps had indeed revived the tragedy but the sun was shining and the air was warm. The massed beds of roses were showing green shoots; a few more weeks and they would be in all their glory.

As I entered the house, a footman approached me. 'There's a gentleman in the library, Miss Sophia. He would give no name. Said you were expecting him.'

I thanked him in what I hoped was a normal voice and followed him decorously, praying that he would not notice the colour that had rushed to my face. My heart was racing, so that I thought I should cease to breathe, for I knew full well the identity of my visitor.

Inside the door, I paused, striving to calm myself. Julian Masters, handsome and devastating as ever, faced me, his back to the fire. For a moment, we gazed in mutual rapture. Then the fetters snapped and at the same moment, we both moved towards each other and I was enfolded in his arms, feeling such security. Gently, he released me, but holding both my hands, gazed earnestly into my face.

'Is it the same with you, Sophia?'

For answer, I unashamedly again sought the sanctuary of his arms but this time, he lifted my face and kissed my lips.

Momentarily I was disappointed, for the kiss lacked that fiery passion that George's kisses by the lakeside had held, but then Julian was leading me over to a windowseat, facing across the vast lawns and the undulating meadows that reached far to the horizon; all belonging now to George, his arm around me, explaining, 'I could not come earlier . . . the storms . . . my business affairs. Yet I am glad that we have both had time . . .'

'But you know nothing of me, sir, except that I was Lady Perriman's ward.'

'There is nothing I want to know. All I want is your promise to marry me . . .'

'But, Julian . . .' As I falteringly

spoke his name for the first time he again took me in his arms, again kissing me but this time the pressure of his lips was much harder.

Releasing myself, I went on, 'I can't marry you . . . yet. There are the children. I am in charge of them until . . . until their brother, George comes home.'

Immediately, he was all contrition. 'Forgive me, Sophia. I am indeed selfish, thinking only of myself, not asking what arrangements have been made . . . '

I told him everything except about my legacy. At that moment it seemed so irrelevant.

He gave a sigh. 'So I must wait until the new Lord Perriman comes home.' He kissed my hand. 'Well, provided you do not keep me waiting a day longer than necessary, I suppose I must be patient.'

I took a deep breath. 'Julian . . . apart from the care of the children, there . . . there is another reason . . . why . . . why . . . we cannot . . . why we must wait until George comes home.'

'Another reason?'

Hesitatingly, I began, 'The day that George Perriman left to go on foreign service . . . he asked me to be his wife.'

There it was told. I waited. Why didn't Julian speak?

Then, 'And what answer did you give him?'

'I . . . I promised to wait for him . . . but almost as soon as he had gone . . . I had my fears. How could I a nobody, marry someone of such high rank . . . even though I do love him for we were brought up as brother and sister . . . '

'He will understand.' He tried to be jocular. 'Does he now become your guardian? Do I have to ask him for your hand?'

I shivered. There was so much more that Julian would have to be told. He was quick to feel the tremor.

'What pesters you, Sophia? Of what are you afraid?'

Where should I begin? Should I go on evading the truth? I tried to equivocate. 'George . . . George is so . . . so gentle . . . so trusting. I dread the thought of hurting him. By now the news of the tragedy will have reached him . . . he will be almost out of his mind . . . no-one to confide in . . . no-one to comfort him . . . believing in me . . . then to come home . . . and to find that even I . . . '

Julian had taken me by the shoulders, gently turning me so that I was looking out of the window.

'Look out there, Sophia. Look well and take in all that you can see. Marry George Perriman and all that will belong to you. You will be Lady Perriman. You will be the mistress of this beautiful house.' There was a strange hardness in his voice as he went on. 'Although I cannot give you an establishment to compare with this, I am a toleraby rich man. I am building

179

a factory up here in Yorkshire and later I hope to stand for parliament, and by God, Miss Sophia, I know of no woman to compare with you, who could so help further my ambitions.'

'Julian, stop! You must listen to me. There are many things I must tell you. First of all, I am of unknown birth . . . '

'Now I command you to stop, Miss Sophia. What care I? Now let us close the matter, for tomorrow I ride to Leeds to see the foundations of my factory being laid and I do not wish to lose a single moment of your company in fruitless argument. I shall be gone three or four days but with your permission, I shall call on my way back.'

* * *

It was three days since Julian had driven away. Would he return today? Tomorrow? Although I savoured the moment when I should be in his arms again, I had a deep sense of guilt.

He had stayed to dinner, meeting Mr. and Mrs. Long to whom I had introduced him as a friend of the late Lord Perriman adding that both Barbara and I had met him in London. Barbara had been quiet throughout the meal; indeed almost sulky giving but the most meagre of answers whenever he spoke to her. After his departure, she demanded to know the nature of his call. When I protested it was just friendship, her terms of denunciation were most unladylike but I put that down to her youth. I longed to take her into my confidence but how could I expect her to understand something that even I felt nothing but a strange mixture of emotions?

* * *

We had now been in strict mourning for over four months. Surely, I asked Mrs. Long, could we not relax a little? The many hued spring flowers and all the delicate shades of new green seemed to demand it. Mrs. Long was all understanding, suggesting mauve and purple. Without any loss of time, I had Dorcas helping me on with my mauve chiffon and taffeta.

'Lord, Miss Sophia, 'tis now far too vast fitting. Didn't I tell you all along what would happen with eating so little?'

'But you can take it in at the seams, can you not? See.' I nipped in the waist at the same time scanning myself in the tall pier glass.

After all those weeks of sombre black, I appeared to myself as a different person. I liked my new slenderness; my face had fined down, but oh the rapture of once again wearing a pretty gown! I fingered the paniers of delicate material and in that moment, decided that I must wear it that very afternoon. Julian might return and I wanted him to see the butterfly emerged from its chrysalis.

'You can do it, can you not, Dorcas?

Now? Straightaway?'

'Why, yes, Miss Sophia. 'Tis a treat for sore eyes to see you looking so lovely again.'

Stepping out of the dress and throwing on a loose robe, I watched her dexterous fingers. She had more or less taken over from Martha, her only fault being so prone to gathering and passing on gossip. Yet, I had learned, it was the greatest enjoyment of most ladies of quality, so tolerance should be shown when servants merely copied their betters.

I picked up a book and tried to read, but Julian Masters thrust himself on to every page, making concentration impossible so that a knock on the door came as a welcome relief.

It was one of the housemaids, sent up by a footman to say that a Mrs. Barton had called and wished to see Miss Barton.

Mrs. Barton? The only Mrs. Barton I knew of was the woman who had fostered me as a small child . . . and she was dead. I pulled myself together and told the girl that although I was now engaged in dressing, I would be down as quickly as possible. I didn't want to hurry. I was suddenly afraid to meet the woman, but Dorcas, as became a good maid, was purposefully making haste and within a few minutes was slipping the dress over my head.

It was a perfect fit, emphasising my new figure; the shade suiting my red-gold curls but when I looked in the glass I was shocked at the pallor of my cheeks, instinctively reaching for the Spanish wool.

'Not too much, Miss Sophia. A delicate pallor is more becoming for your hair colour.'

I was playing for time. 'I would like a ribbon, Dorcas. The same shade as the dress.'

I seated myself before the dressing-table watching as she tied it . . . then suggesting that I would like the bow higher until I could delay the moment no longer. As I walked slowly down the grand staircase towards the library, my mind was in complete bewilderment, for puzzles were crowding in on me. Who was this woman? How did she know of me? Why was she asking for me?

The footman held the door open but when it had closed behind me, I stood rooted to the spot. Seated, watching my entrance was the well remembered, uncouth, unprepossessing, obese figure of Mrs. Mathews, from Curton Workhouse. Her face wore an expression of avid malignant glee. She made no effort to rise and greet me, as I stood there speechless, my thoughts frozen my legs immobile. Then her obscene cackle startled me. 'Then you do remember me . . . me who mothered you when Mrs. Barton died? Now Mathews is dead and I'm married to Ned Barton. Come, come, have you no greeting for me after all these years?'

I could hardly recognise my croaking voice. 'Why are you here?' How did you know where . . . ?'

'One question at a time. My, my, that's a handsome gown you're a-wearing! That must have cost a pretty penny . . . '

'Will you please come to the point, ma'am . . . '

'Oh, oh, so the fine lady goes all haughty . . . and me who nurtured you when you could have starved to death. Well, it all began when I read of a terrible double riding tragedy. Poor things, I said to myself. It makes no difference whether you're a titled lady or a mere minder of workhouse brats. When the Lord calls you, you've got to go. Then I noticed the name. Perriman. Why, that was the very lady who took little Sophia Barton into her service. Nice little thing, Sophia. I was sorry to see her go . . . '

'Mrs. Barton,' I interrupted. 'I see no purpose in all this talk.' By now, I was more in command of myself and there was a hint of hauteur in my voice. I went to the door, holding it wide open. As she made no attempt to move, I said peremptorily, 'Will you please go, or must I call a servant?'

There was a malevolence in her voice. 'Don't you come the ugly with me, my jumped-up workhouse brat. I'm the one that has the information . . . information that others would relish to get hold of.'

Helpless before her gloating eyes, my hand slackened on the doorknob and I found myself slowly walking back and sitting in an opposite chair.

'That's more like it. Now we can talk. Where was I? Oh, yes. Lord and Lady Perriman both dead. Then a couple of weeks later I read an account of the funeral, together with list of mourners and blow me, you could have knocked me to the ground with a feather, when I see, 'Miss Sophia Barton' ward of the late Lord and Lady Perriman. Now just how did you manage that dearie?'

My mind was whirling in confusion. I could not think of what to say but the taunting voice went on remorselessly.

'Poor little Sophia Barton . . . never knew her mother did she?'

'My mother? You know of her? Tell me . . . '

'Not so much of a hurry, Miss Sophia. How much are you prepared to pay?'

'Pay? I have no money . . . '

'Bah! Don't tell me that. I'll warrant you have some pretty pieces of jewellery . . . '

She eyed me narrowly. 'You know of course,' she said slowly, 'there are others who'll be willing to pay . . . '

'Others? Who?'

'The Perrimans of course.' Her voice took on a wheedling tone, 'But come now dearie, you're the one who should know the truth about your birth.'

I felt a strange tightness in my throat. Of course I wanted to know for good or ill to be able to tell George . . . and Julian . . . but most of all for my own satisfaction.

'Now dearie, how about that bracelet?' She heaved herself from the chair and came over to me as though to remove it from my wrist. I recoiled in horror at the thought of her touching me but at the same time, I undid the clasp and handed it over.

She held it up so that the light caught the jewels and then dropped it into her dilapidated reticule, once again seating herself.

'Well, to cut a long story short, after reading the funeral notice I tried to quiz Ned about you, but he wasn't talking . . . not until I'd got him well and truly soaked. Come to think of it Miss Barton, you're a poor one, not offering a drink to a lady.'

I went over and began to pour a glass of madeira. 'Not that thin stuff. I like something with some body in it. Rum . . . or brandy . . . or gin.'

I handed her a glass of brandy which she drank in almost one gulp, causing her to catch her breath and then to belch loudly.

'That's better. Much better. Well, when Ned got talking, there he was, telling me of the night you arrived, that old Nannie Martha, carrying you wrapped like an Egyptian mummy . . . '

'Martha took me to Mrs. Barton?' I asked incredulously.

'That's right. Now you're catching on. Can't you guess the rest?'

I felt dizzy. My brain was spinning. 'You mean . . . ?'

'I mean that Lady Perriman was your mother . . . '

'Stop!' I almost screamed the word.

'Shame that she never told you herself . . . nor that silly old nanny-goat. I was talking to her before you came down. Admitted every word I said . . . '

'But why? And my father? Who was he?'

'Your guess is as good as mine,' came the sneering retort, 'but we both know the outcome. When Lady Perriman, your dear loving mamma, was ready, she came and removed you. Oh don't look so shocked; accidents happen in the best of families,' and again the

190

horrible laughter filled the room.

'But why?' I again began . . .

'Why, why, why' she mimicked. 'Do you think a fine gentleman, like Lord Perriman would have married her, if he'd known about you? Ask the old woman, about the bastard she took to the Barton's . . . she knows all the answers.'

How soon, I wondered could I get rid of this loathsome creature and go to Martha . . . to insist she told me everything.

As though reading my thoughts, she clumsily rose to her feet. 'I have a hired carriage waiting. I thought I could well afford the luxury, though I'm mighty disappointed, you've paid so ill for the information. Still, there's always another day, workhouse brat.'

As she left the room, I closed my eyes so that I should not see her pass before me. The confusion within me was so great, I did not know which way to turn. I must go to Martha. When I opened my eyes, I found myself looking at Julian Masters, who had come in through the French window. How much, oh God, how much had he heard.

For a moment, I stood there, as though paralysed, while by the window, he appeared to be staring at me as though he could not comprehend. How much had he heard? A feeling of utter shame engulfed me. Then the room began to spin round and round . . . I could feel myself about to fall.

When I came to, I was lying on a sofa, with Julian's arm around my shoulder. For a moment, I wished I need never leave the comfort of that caress, then memory came flooding back. I searched his eyes, expecting to find disgust and loathing but there was only tenderness and compassion.

'It's all right, Sophia. Don't talk for a few minutes. She's gone.'

I struggled to sit up. 'You heard what she called me?'

He nodded gravely, 'But there's no need to talk about it, unless . . . '

'What she said is true. Lady Perriman brought me here from a Lancashire Poor Law Institution. I was to be apprenticed in her kitchen. Then . . . '

I stopped as the tremendous knowledge reasserted itself. Lady Perriman was my mother. Had she all along intended that I should be brought up as her ward, not a kitchenmaid? Had George's accident been an act of Providence, to make matters easier?

I had to tell Julian. 'Lady Perriman is . . .' My impetuous voice came to a sudden halt. Had I the right to disclose her secret to a stranger? But then, it was also my secret . . . and I had to confide in someone.

I took a long, deep breath. 'I don't know how much you heard but I want to tell you everything, knowing that you will tell no other living soul.'

He nodded gravely. 'You have my word of honour, Miss Sophia.'

How could I begin? There was only one way. 'That . . . that person was from the . . . the workhouse.

193

She . . . she came to tell me that . . . that Lady Perriman was my mother.'

There it was out. Julian Masters' face was inscrutable but before he could speak, I was babbling out all I knew.

He let me talk; sometimes clearly at others almost incoherently, never once interrupting, until I breathlessly came to an end. Why doesn't he say something, I wondered frantically . . . and then I saw the half frown, half smile on his face as he slowly said, 'Don't you see what this means Sophia? You can't marry George Perriman. He is your step-brother!'

Why hadn't I thought of that? Truth to tell, George had been far from my thoughts. Of course he would immediately see that we couldn't marry but wouldn't the telling of his mother's youthful folly be hurtful to his gentle nature?

I shook myself. 'I don't know that we should tell George. Wouldn't it be better to leave him in ignorance about his mother? Tell him that I . . . I have had a . . . change of heart?'

'No, Sophia, I think not. I have lived long enough to learn that it is far better to know and face up to the truth, however unpleasant it might be. In this way, he would not know or think you unfaithful. Again, what is there to prevent that woman telling him . . . blackmailing him? Believe me, my love, George will be man enough to understand. He had, I believe a great feeling for his mother?'

'They adored each other . . . '

'Then you need have no fear . . . '

'Julian' I was on my feet. 'That woman told me she had spoken to Martha. I must go to her. She is so weak these days, so easily distressed. Pray help yourself to the madeira while I am gone.'

I sped upstairs to Martha's small sitting-room. She was not there. I tried both Barbara's and my room finally going up to the next landing where she had her bedroom. I made to open the door but it would only move a few inches. There was something behind that door, on the floor. I knelt down and put my hand through the aperture. I could feel something . . . Martha's inert body. I again tried to move the door but it would go no further and fearing that more forceful pushing might hurt her, I raced down-stairs, back to the library.

Gasping out my story, Julian interrupted. 'Pull the bell and order a ladder to the window. If it is fastened, tell them to break the glass.'

He followed me upstairs but he wouldn't take the risk of using his strength being unable to see just what was Martha's condition nor how she was stretched out.

'Oh, how I wish they would hurry, hurry, hurry,' I breathed.

'I'll go, my sweet. You stay here, ready to attend Martha as soon as I open the door.'

He was gone, pushing his way

through the group of servants who had gathered round on hearing the commotion. Then with relief, I heard the tinkle of breaking glass. Julian's quick footsteps, a few, long drawn out seconds and then, 'You can get in now' and pushing open the door, I was just in time to see Julian placing Martha on her bed.

I was on my knees instantly. She neither spoke nor moved. Dorcas and some of the maids had followed me in.

'Quick! The smelling-salts . . . and some hot-water bottles. She's icy cold. There's no telling how long she had been on the floor.' Julian's voice was firm and commanding. 'Then everyone else, outside.'

'She is alive?' I asked fearfully.

'Of a certainty. Ah, here are the smelling-salts. They should bring her round.'

I watched with bated breath. What, on seeing me, would be her first words? I put the hot bottles at her feet and one on either side. Still, there was no response . . . then a feeble flutter of her eye-lids.

I slipped my hand under the covers and sought hers. It was still cold. I pressed and rubbed it. The eye-lids fluttered again.

'Martha . . . it's Sophia.'

Her eyes, now open, just stared fixedly ahead.

'Martha . . . can you hear me? It's Sophia.'

There was just the merest of movements of her head as though to indicate she had heard. Julian, from the other side of the bed, slipped by me, whispering, 'We must send for the doctor.'

I continued to sit there, frantic as to Martha's silence. Why didn't she speak? I ordered that a dish of tea should be brought and with great difficulty Dorcas and I managed to get a little down her throat but she seemed to have lost all movement . . . and her speech.

Oh, God, I prayed, do something

for Martha but I knew that actually I was praying for myself. If Martha died without speaking, I should never know the truth of my birth.

Why was Julian so long but when he did come back he brought the doctor with him, having driven down to the village himself.

The doctor's diagnosis was brief. Martha was suffering from a stroke, resulting no doubt from the delayed shock of the tragedy. It might not be of long duration; on the other hand . . . He shrugged his shoulders. She would not necessarily die . . . yet. Her heart was strong, but whether she would ever get back full use of her limbs and her speech, time alone could tell.

Shock of the tragedy! I knew different. It was the horror of what that woman had said to her . . . reviving the memory of my birth . . . the agony of my mother's mind and body, for Martha was devoted to her.

It was then that I determined I would

nurse her, so I should be there the instant her speech came back. She was sleeping now, the doctor having given her an opiate, so Julian and I returned to the library to say our farewell.

He insisted I sat down while he poured two glasses of wine. 'Sophia, I wish I did not have to leave you. You are over-taxing yourself. First that horrible visit today, and now an invalid on your hands. But come, let us drink to the future.'

I did not raise my glass but put it down on a near side-table and asked dully, 'What is going to happen next?' The future seems so dark.'

'You are going to marry me. Would to God we would marry straightaway then you would know that whatever happened, nothing could hurt you for I should be there to shoulder the burden.'

Listening to him, I was aware of his goodness and sincerity but my bemused mind was wandering in many directions.

'Do you think, sir, do you think she would ever have told me . . . that . . . that she was my . . . my mother?'

He shook his head. ' 'Tis hard to say. It would have had its dangers. From what you have told me, she had built up a security about your relationship. She was giving you a mother's love but having kept her secret all these years, she could not now tell her husband.'

I knew he spoke wisely but oh, what joy it would have been to have flung my arms around her with real childish abandonment and called her 'Mama' instead of the well brought-up ward who kissed her dear Aunt Lucy with true affection because she was grateful for her love.

As though, lost in my self-pity, I was startled to hear him continue. 'I too, never knew my mother.'

'I am indeed truly sorry, sir,'

'She died at my birth. My grandparents brought me up. 'Tis my grandfather's business that I have inherited . . . '

'But your father?'

'He married again. I have nothing to complain about. I had a happy childhood, a good education. My grandmother was kind and loving . . . but like you, . . . I have often wished.' For a moment, his voice died away and then, 'Come, Sophia. Drink your wine. I want to see the bloom come back into your cheeks.'

Obediently, I drank but Julian did not repeat the toast. Perhaps, I thought miserably, he too can see the future through a dark and murky glass.

He had taken both my hands in his. 'Now listen, Sophia. If George should return before I come north again, send for me immediately. Once he is home, I would not waste another moment away from you . . . and should anything happen to Martha . . . again send for me, for I know that you will then be so desolate.' He kissed me gently. 'Promise me, Sophia.'

I nodded mutely, the only reply I could make, for now the time for parting had come, I felt I could not bear to let him go, so brief, yet so pregnant with calamities, had been our meeting. I had an overbearing sense of more sorrow to come, yet, I could not ask him to stay. He had his business to see to, but more important still, he had no real right in the Perriman household, to allow him to stay. Indeed, up in Martha's bedroom, when he was giving his quickfire orders, I had seen raised eyebrows and odd looks being passed between the servants.

He had walked up from the village, so I suggested that I accompanied him as far as the lodge gates. We walked along, my hand through his arm, as any betrothed girl would do, but neither of us speaking a word.

We met Barbara and the other children, returning from their riding. We stopped to talk for a moment, telling them of Martha's illness, and warning the little ones not to make a noise or go into her room. Barbara was silent, barely civil, as though she resented Julian's presence. Or was it because Charles noticed my light-coloured dress, and stroking it, murmured, 'Pretty, Pretty.'

As we moved on, I apologised for myself. 'Perhaps I did wrong in wearing this dress — coming out of mourning so soon . . .'

'You look adorable in it, Sophia. This mourning etiquette is too severe. I'm sure Lady Lucy . . . and Lord Hugh much prefer to see you looking gay.'

We had reached the lodge gate. Gently he took me in his arms, and kissed me, but the kiss was hard, so that my lips felt bruised. 'After George comes home, there'll ne no more partings,' he murmured. 'We'll get a special licence. In the meantime, dear heart, I will write to you . . . and you'll write to me?'

'Oh, yes Julian, yes. Why didn't we think of writing before?'

'Because I wished that you should have time to consider . . . without being persuaded by ardent, adoring letters.'

We kissed again. This time a tender salute of farewell.

'Now back you go, dear heart.' He took me by the shoulders; turning me to face the house. 'Don't look round.' I began to walk. I heard the clang of the big, iron gate. I knew that he had gone, but I walked on without looking back. Somehow Julian Masters, even in his gentleness, commanded obedience.

Reaching my room, I abandoned myself to the torrent of tears I had so long been holding back. Then becoming calmer, I tried to fathom out my exact position; how much should I tell Mary and Barbara but every direct line of action eluded me, my thoughts being in such a state of contradiction.

I was attempting to remove traces of my weeping when Barbara came into the room.

'La, Sophia, weeping because your lover had gone?' There was childish sarcasm in her voice. 'Why has that man been here again? Dorcas tells me that he was in Martha's bedroom. Are you partial to him?'

The blunt question on top of all the afternoon's distress unnerved me and I spoke more sharply than I intended.

'It so happens that I am, but it is no business of yours . . . '

'Is it not? Then I shall tell Mary and she will tell Grandmother Perriman . . . '

'Barbara! We are all getting so edgy and cross with one another . . . we have been through such an unhappy time . . . '

'Not you, flaunting your chance acquaintances . . . making love in my father's house so that all the servants are talking . . . '

'Stop it, Barbara,' I shouted.

' . . . and wearing that dress . . . '
She was now weeping noisily.

'I'm sorry about that, I'll go and change immediately . . . '

'No . . . no. I didn't mean that. I . . . I . . . ' Her sobbing became louder.

206

'I . . . I . . . I would like to wear a pretty frock . . . '

I put my arm around her. 'And so you shall. We'll choose a dress this very moment.'

I went and put an arm around her but she pettishly shook me away and dashed out of the room.

How horrible it was all becoming. As children, we had squabbled, got into pelters with one another, fallen into mops and fits of sullens, but there was no malice behind the temporary upsets, for we soon kissed and were friends again. Now there was an alien tension in the air.

How ironical, I thought, that this discord should come about today of all days . . . the day, I had learned that the Perriman children were my half brothers and sisters.

7

Any day now, a carriage, travelling swiftly, its' horses foam-flecked, would come dashing up the long avenue, stop in front of the main entrance and Lord George Perriman would step out to claim his heritage.

Each morning, my first waking thoughts would visualise the picture and rehearse what I should say. There was so much to tell and I tormented myself as to how it should be told without adding to the existing grief.

Then I would remember Martha and would dash to her room wondering if there had been any overnight change in her condition.

For the first few days, I had insisted on nursing her myself, but the doctor, noticing my exhausted condition due to little sleep or proper meals pointed out my folly, and he himself arranged for a nurse and a relay of servants to sit with her day and night. 'Please God,' I would pray, 'Don't let her die, without telling me of my father . . . and the mystery surrounding my birth . . . and Lady Perriman . . . my mother.'

My mother. What a wealth of love went into those two words . . . words that could now never be spoken directly. Yet, when I most keenly felt the loss, I would remember Julian shared the same sorrow and it was another bond between us.

Since his return to London, he had written me several times, confiding his hopes and ambitions. The shipping and export business that he had inherited from his grandfather brought him a good income but meeting cloth merchants, exporting woollen goods had inspired him to come north, build his own factory and employ his own weavers for who he intended to build decent cottages in place of the existing hovels. As soon as he was established and had won a worthwhile reputation, he hoped to stand for parliament. In the meantime, we would be married having found ourselves a suitable estate in the Yorkshire countryside within easy access of his mill. Did these plans meet with my approval?

I was quick to write back extolling his ambitions but demanding that he employed no child-labour under ten years of age. I could so well remember seven-year olds, being taken daily from the workhouse and brought back at night scarcely able to lift their feet from the ground and falling asleep over their scanty supper.

Our exchange of letters drew us closer; made us more aware of each other's character and for me they made the waiting endurable.

Martha was showing signs of improvement. She could now turn her head with apparent greater ease, and in answer to straightforward questions . . . 'would she like a drink' . . . 'was she tired' . . . she could nod or shake her head. The doctor, however, warned us not to tax her strength with too many questions, as any excitement could be fatal. Each day I would sit by her bedside, holding her poor paralysed hand and talk of the children's coming and goings, with an occasional nod from her, or if relating a piece of mischief, a tiny head-shake. I always finished my chat with a cheery, 'Well Martha, who knows, Master George might be home today,' and I'll swear, these last few days, I had felt a little pressure from her hand.

This morning, it was pouring with rain when I awoke. For a moment I pondered on the day's forthcoming activities. Riding, always the high-light of the children's day was, out of the question. 'No riding today' was the most dreaded punishment for laziness in the schoolroom, or indeed for any misdemeanour. Now I would have to think of some divertissement for them, but in the meantime, I must be about my daily routine.

Throwing on a light wrapper, I made

my way to Martha's room, bidding the woman she could go, and that I would wait until her relief came. There was a smile on Martha's face. I asked if she had slept well and received a nod. Would she like a drink? Another nod, and as I put the feeding cup to her lips, she pursed her mouth, making a hissing noise.

'You're trying to say, 'Sophy', I exclaimed excitedly.

She nodded.

'Try again,' I urged.

Again the hissing sound. Nothing more, but now I felt sure that Martha would eventually recover her speech. I put down the feeding cup. 'I must go and dress now. Who knows, George might come home today.'

A semblance of a smile hovered about her mouth. Another sound. Was she trying to say 'George'?

We had now reached the stage of wearing half-mourning; the little girls in white and the grown ups in every conceivable shade of mauve and purple and grey. On a dull morning such as this, I decided I needed to wear something in definite contrast, finally settling on a white muslin, sprigged with lilac. I went to see the children in the schoolroom. They had already breakfasted and were busy with their French verbs, Mam'selle scolding because they were paying more attention to the rain than to correct pronunciation. I tried to cheer them up, saying that if the rain ceased they could go riding as usual.

The rain did not cease. The children were disconsolate. I was at my wits' end as to how to keep them amused. They had their toys but a rainy day is so depressing that even old favourites are rejected.

'I know. We'll have a party up here in the schoolroom. I'll get Mrs. Groves to send up sandwiches, pastries and cakes . . . perhaps a jelly and whim-wham. You can put on party dresses and ribbons in your hair as if you were really entertaining, and Charles can wear his new blue velvet suit.'

That I thought, would occupy a little of the afternoon, but before long they were back surrounding me, demanding, 'Now what shall we do?'

I regarded them wistfully. Elizabeth. Caroline. Charles. I was their half-sister. It was my duty to give them my love and care. Barbara, since her outburst on the occasion of Julian's last visit, had taken herself off to stay with Mary and her husband at their not-too-far-away mansion. Actually, they had arranged this with Grandmother Perriman for she was almost ready to make her entrance into society but until then, she had demurred, saying she wanted to be at home when George arrived. I was not sorry to see her go for she was having a disturbing influence on her younger sisters.

We began the party quietly, with absolute decorum. The children, even baby Charles had had some dancing lessons, so with me at the schoolroom piano, I suggested they should show me how they were progressing. All went well for a while until they began arguing among themselves as to who were making false steps, so then we went on to simple musical games and soon the room was filled with a riot of happy noises. As the noise increased, I found myself, instead of disciplining the children, actually inciting them to make more, banging louder and louder on the piano for in doing so I began to feel my spirits rise, ridding myself of all the past months' repressions.

At last, however, I had to call a halt suggesting that we took a rest to get back our breath. Down they flopped on the floor, laughing and rolling around with a total absence of well brought-up deportment. It was a blessing that the schoolroom was at the top of the house and I almost laughed aloud as I thought of what Martha would have said could she have seen them. I could not scold, for I myself felt so elated, so carefree.

'More play,' demanded Charles,

coming over and tugging at my hand.

'I know,' suggested Elizabeth, 'Let's play Blind Man's Buff,' and taking the silk sash from her dress, tied it over her eyes. What a mad scramble! Chairs and stools were overturned but as no-one was hurt, the game had to go on until everybody had been blind-man.

'Now Sophy!' It was Charles again, never showing any sign of fatigue; always to the fore with bright ideas. I allowed them to tie the ribbon around my eyes and heard them scatter in all directions. Cautiously, I felt my way around tables and chairs, hands outstretched, hoping to catch a victim. Suddenly their squeals subsided. What had happened? I tried to pull off the sash but it had knotted and was tight round my head. Then I found myself in two strong arms, a man's face against mine, and that well remembered voice murmuring, 'Sophy, Sophy.'

Now the squealing had broken loose again. 'It's George. It's George. George has come home,' as George himself removed the sash and looked into my eyes.

He drew me to him and kissed me tenderly on each cheek, murmuring, 'Little Sophy, my own dear little Sophy . . . ' and then he had Charles in his arms and a sister hanging at each side, all demanding to be hugged and kissed again and again, until freeing himself, he took my two hands standing back in appraisal, murmuring. 'You are more beautiful than ever.'

When he would have drawn me to him, I gently pushed him away, whispering, 'Not now, George,' then in a louder voice, 'How long have you been here? We didn't hear your carriage.'

'Little wonder,' he laughed, 'considering the noise you were making. When I was told you were all up here, well, up I dashed.'

He had changed. He was taller and broader; more masculine; more sure of himself and his well-cut jacket and breeches gave him the air of a smart man-about-town. He caught me looking at him. 'Yes, was I not fortunate that my father's tailor had some ready-mades that actually fit me?'

I tried to recall that feeling of elation that only a short while ago had sent my spirits soaring, but it had fled. Nevertheless, I attempted to infuse some gaiety into my voice. 'Very handsome, sir, but now we must go down. The servants will wish to greet you . . . a messenger must be sent to Mary and Barbara . . . we must invite them to dinner . . . ' I stopped as I realised my excitement was getting the upper hand, 'I'm sorry, George. Now you are home, you must give the orders. Forget everything I've said and make whatever arrangements are most pleasing to you.'

'Nonsense, Sophy. I'm deeply grateful for your thought and practical consideration. I called on Mr. Stevens as soon as I reached London and he told me how you were here in charge of the family. We are all much indebted to you, Sophy,' then hoisting Charles on to his shoulder. 'Downstairs we go then, and let's get the fuss over and done with.'

Mustered in the hall were all the members of the household staff, headed by Mr. Long and the butler, both of whom spoke formal yet warm greetings to their young, new master. For the first time, I saw the shadow cross George's face, but in an instant it was gone, as, with a few words of thanks, he led the way into the library, only to suddenly wheel round and demand, 'Martha? Where is Martha? Don't tell me she too . . .'

Hastily I told him of her condition.

'When can I see her?'

'She usually sleeps in the afternoon but later . . .'

Charles was now indignantly making himself heard, 'We were having a party . . .'

'Yes, a party! You couldn't have chosen a better day and I haven't eaten for hours,' laughed George.

'How remiss of me.' I pulled the bell and asked that the cakes and sweetmeats should now be served in the library, with something more substantial for George, but he had little opportunity for eating, the children plying him with question after question.

For my part, my mind was engrossed as to what and how much I was going to tell him when the moment of reckoning came. With the first gong for dressing, I ushered the little ones back upstairs, handing them over to their nurses. They would be in their beds long before dinner was served, the meal being put off until Mary and Barbara arrived.

I had been in my room for only a few minutes when there was a discreet tap on the door. I knew it to be George. I called to him to enter. Closing the door behind him, he stood regarding me a look of the happy victor on his face. Then he strode over and his arms were around me, kissing me again and again with complete abandonment, and when

I would have returned the caresses as his lips demanded, it suddenly crashed down on me with horror, 'This is your brother . . . your brother! He was quick to notice my reluctance. 'What is it Sophy? We are betrothed. Now I can announce it to the whole world . . . '

'No, George. No.' I interrupted.

His arms slackened as a look of bewilderment and pain crossed his face. 'No, no, I am not the right person to be Lady Perriman . . . '

He laughed in relief. 'Is that all that pesters you? Oh Sophy, for a moment you had me scared . . . that you had found another love. Not the right person to step into my mother's shoes? Mama would have preferred you to all others.'

He moved to take me in his arms again, but I moved quickly aside. 'George you must listen to me. I . . . I . . . there is someone else.'

I was horrified at the ashen-hue that came over his face. For a moment, he stared speechless, then, 'I don't believe it Sophy. You are trying to make kind of an excuse . . . ' Then as I didn't reply ' . . . you of all people . . . you Sophy . . . my beloved companion of all those years.'

I had to say something. Feverishly, I attempted, ' . . . But don't you see, George, that was the root of the trouble. Neither you nor I have met but few others . . . '

'It would appear you were quick to meet another,' he broke in brutally, ' . . . and quick to favour him with your affection . . . '

'No, George, it was not like that . . . '

'Who is he? Do I know him?'

'No, I think not, but your father brought him here on the night of your farewell assembly . . . '

'That man! That thieving, robbing scoundrel!' The force of his explosive anger alarmed me. ' . . . Not only has he ruined my father by coercing him to join in hare-brained factory schemes, but he has also, in my absence, stolen my betrothed wife. I shall call him out. It is a vile insult . . . not to be tolerated.'

'George, please calm down. Let me explain.' It was as though we were back in the schoolroom with George in a childish pelter, but I had not reckoned with George, the man, the new Lord Perriman.

'I have no wish to hear your explanations,' he said coldly, 'I called on Mr. Stevens and he told me of the sorry affairs of the Perriman estate . . . almost bankrupt. Did your precious lover tell you that? How he had wheedled from my father his last few thousands? It was good for him that he was out of town at the time, but Mr. Stevens has promised that he will bring him up here the moment he returns. Now I am looking forward to meeting him with double relish and I care not what the outcome may be.' For an instant, words failed him, then shaking his head in dejection, 'That I should have such a welcome . . . the first day of my return, to hear that you,

Sophy, could not wait for me.'

I could find no words with which to reply for all that would come to my mind, was that here, facing me, angry and disappointed was my beloved step-brother. Should I tell him? He would then at least understand why I could not marry him, but would not the knowledge of my birth distress him still more?

I was spared the anguish of making a decision by his asking in a dull voice, 'Have we time to see Martha before dinner?'

Glad of the reprieve, I hastily stammered, 'Why, yes . . . better now . . . later on she'll be asleep . . . she spends much time sleeping.' As we reached the bedroom, I paused for a moment. 'She can understand what we say, so please George, do not say anything that might excite her.'

He nodded and followed me into the room. Bending over the bed, I said softly. 'Martha, Master George has come home. He is here.'

Slowly her eyes opened. She made as though to lift her arms, but George bent down quickly and kissed her on both cheeks. She was trying to speak but only harsh croaking sounds escaped while she repeatedly nodded her head first at George and then at me.

We didn't stay long, assuring her that we would both visit her again in the morning. As I left the room, I asked the woman waiting outside, to be sure to give her an opiate, fearing the excitement of seeing George, might result in a restless night.

'Does the doctor hold out any hope for her recovery,' he asked as we walked along the corridor;

'Not full recovery. She will be bedridden for the rest of her life, but the doctor says her brain, apart from her speech is perfectly sound.'

'Poor Martha. Always so active. It must be torment for her. She and my mother were devoted to each other, even though they were mistress and maid.'

It was fortunate that we had reached my room, for again I was tempted to tell him of the tragic bond that inspired that devotion, but with a mere inclination of his head, he opened my door and stood aside for me to enter.

Dorcas was waiting for me and within seconds, I was seated at my dressing-table while she brushed, combed and twisted my curls into position.

'Miss Mary and Miss Barbara have arrived alone; young Sir Henry being away on business until tomorrow, and isn't it odd Miss Sophy, neither of them seem to have a word for the cat . . . just whispering to each other . . . as though they've got a secret. Do you think it could be that Miss Mary is . . . ?'

'Miss Mary never could keep a secret so we shall soon know if that is the case. Oh, I'm glad you brought out the mauve taffeta . . . '

'Well, Miss Sophy, I knew you'd want to look your prettiest tonight of all nights . . . you and Master

George always did make a handsome pair.' She giggled. 'There I go again, calling him Master George instead of Lord Perriman.'

She slipped the dress over my head and as she fastened the hooks and tapes, I pondered as to why she emphasised the association between me and George. How much did she know? Had we been the subject for gossip, rumour and guess-work below stairs?

★ ★ ★

When I entered the drawing-room, Mary and Barbara were engrossed in deep conversation both barely greeting me, beyond Mary demanding, 'Where is George?'

'Here' came the calm voice as he strode over, first kissing one and then the other before standing back giving them a long, cool, look, finally stating 'So . . . one sophisticated matron and the other a delightful, seductive looking little filly.'

'George!' Barbara's girlish squeal filled the room as she possessively took one arm and Mary the other, 'You would never have dared to say such things before . . . '

'No, little sister, being a belted earl gives a man many privileges.' Slowly I followed them into the dining-room.

Throughout the meal, they bombarded him with a barrage of questions, he giving them quick-fire answers leaving me no chance to join in, but back in the drawing-room with our coffee, he said unexpectedly, 'Now I've done enough talking. You begin, Mary and tell me about your wedding-day. Then Sophy, you tell me of the next day . . . '

' . . . and I'll tell you what happened after that,' broke in Barbara venomously.

In a low voice, Mary related the highlights of her wedding day, and I was glad when she mentioned the apparent tenderness between their parents. 'Indeed, I cannot remember Papa and Mama being so happy together, and Papa had already arranged to stay for Christmas . . . '

She could not go on. George looked towards me. I began by telling him of the parade . . . how I took the children to see the horses and the vehicles. I told him of the return.

Both Mary and Barbara were weeping and the tears were running down George's cheeks. Only I remained dry-eyed. I had a horrible cold feeling of impending disaster.

' . . . and at the funeral, Sophy was with a strange man . . . ' It was Barbara, vehemently jerking out the words.

I felt, rather than saw George's eyes upon me. 'He . . . he was an acquaintance of Lord Perriman,' I volunteered.

'But he's been here several times to see you,' retorted Barbara.

I looked at George and was thankful for his understanding. He turned to his sister, saying quietly, 'Sophy is old enough to entertain gentlemen, if she so wishes.'

'But that's not everything. There's something else you should know. I've told Mary, and she says I must tell you . . . that it's not tale-telling or gossip . . . but . . . but that it's important to the family . . .'

Mary could keep me in the background no longer. 'When Barbara first told me, I was shocked . . . horrified. I wanted to come here and confront her . . . Sophy . . . straightway, but Henry advised we should wait until you returned . . .'

My heart bled for George; He looked so completely bewildered.

'All right, then, let's hear it.' He stirred the fire with his boot, sending up a shower of sparks. 'The sooner, I'm in the picture of all that's been happening, the sooner I can take over.'

Still Barbara hesitated. 'I know that you will be angry, I was eavesdropping but I had just returned from riding and passing the library . . . I heard voices . . . the door was open . . . and I heard her say . . .'

'Heard who? Who are you talking about?' George demanded.

'Sophy . . . and a horrible . . . horrible old woman who had called on her . . . '

'Then I forbid you to continue. I don't want to hear any more. Sophy's callers are no concern of ours . . . '

'But this does concern us . . . you . . . all of us.' Mary's voice was shrill with angry excitement.

George looked at me questioningly. Suddenly I felt reckless. I felt I no longer cared what happened. 'Go on, Barbara. If you've told Mary, surely George has a right to know.'

Without looking at me, she began in a muffled voice, 'She said all manner of dreadful things . . . about Mama . . . about a baby . . . '

George's gaze went from one to the other of us. 'What is she talking about? The child's demented. It's all been too much for her.'

I could bear it no longer. 'No, George, what Barbara is trying to tell you, is true.' I was amazed at the steadiness of my voice.

Mary had risen to her feet. There was fury in her voice as she shouted, 'We demand that Sophy tells us everything. Everything.'

Barbara, however, had not finished. 'Then that man came through the French window . . . after the woman had gone. I was still outside the library and the door was still open and I saw them kiss . . . '

She paused to see what effect this information had on her brother, but George's stony stare never relaxed. 'Then they talked and I heard him say, 'but don't you see, you can't marry George Perriman now. You're his step-sister.''

Mary groaned. 'It's not to be tolerated! It's too, too devastating.' Suddenly she turned to me, ' . . . and what is this folly about marrying George? So you fancied yourself as Lady Perriman?'

'Enough, Mary. I will not have Sophy insulted. I may as well tell you, that before sailing for India, I asked Sophy to marry me . . . to wait for my return . . . '

'Lawdy! Lawdy! Lawdy!' Her sarcastic laughter echoed round the room. 'So much for her waiting. Almost as soon as you had sailed, she had taken another lover . . . and now she claims to be our step-sister. La, I have heard some fairy-tales in my time but this beats them all.'

I tried to defend myself. 'I only know what the woman told me.'

I looked at them. Once my dearly-loved friends . . . George totally unable to comprehend the situation . . . Mary and Barbara scornful and arrogant. 'Would you, George, wish to hear all she told me?'

'If it concerns Mamma . . . '

Calmly, I related my story from the time Lady Perriman and Martha had removed me from the workhouse. I repeated, as far as I could remember, word for word of Mrs. Barton's story. I told them of my acquaintance with

Julian Masters and how it had come about.

When I ended, George jumped to his feet in agitation and began walking about the room, stopping occasionally to shake his head, 'My poor darling Mama. How she must have suffered!'

'Suffered? How could she have been so stupid?' stormed Mary, ' . . . and how could she have been so base to deceive Papa all these years?'

'You should not accuse her . . . blame her . . . now that she is dead,' I flashed angrily.

'All very well for you,' was the jeering retort, 'You have cause to be grateful for not being left to rot in the workhouse. You naturally have something to thank her for . . . '

'Stop it! All of you! I will not have this, my mother's drawing-room turned into a barrack-square! Sophy has told us the truth. Of that I am sure. Mama always did love her as a daughter. Now we know why.'

'But after this woman's visit, why

did she not confide in me?' Mary was still suffering from outraged dignity. 'Suppose Barbara had not listened at that open door, we should have been left in complete darkness until she was ready to tell us . . . perhaps to blackmail us . . . '

'Mary! say one more uncharitable word and I shall insist you leave us. Is there anything else you wish to say, Sophy?'

I took a deep breath. 'Yes, I would like to answer Mary. You George, was coming home, expecting to marry me. When Mr. Masters honoured me with his proposal, I rejoiced, for here was a way to break the vow between us, rather than tell of what I had learned, betraying Lady Perriman's secret.'

'But it is sure to get noised abroad. Gossip travels so quickly. We shall be the main topic of every drawing-room of the country.' There was a positive wail in Mary's voice.

'Who will spread the gossip?' I demanded. 'You need have no fear on my part. I too, cherish the memory of my . . . of Lady Perriman.'

George's voice, cold and hard, came across the room. ' 'Tis not pleasant hearing for any of us, therefore, I forbid you to discuss it. I accept every word of the story and I expect all of you to do likewise. Now I think, for all our sakes, we should say goodnight, but for the love of God, be as you were before, in your love for each other.'

But I knew we should never be the same again. I had lost all feeling of security. The Perrimans no longer trusted me, treating me as though I was a cuckoo in the nest. If only Martha would recover her speech. I wanted to know the whole story.

★ ★ ★

There was an air of bitterness; of brooding hanging over the house such as I had never known before. I did not go down to either breakfast or lunch feeling that I could not endure the hostile arrogance of my stepsisters. Last night, they had made me feel unclean, thrusting me back into the mud of Curton.

George, I learned, had spent most of the day in the company of the estate agent, visiting some of the farms and inspecting the new forestry plantations; one of Aunt Lucy's latest ideas for improving the prosperity of Perriman.

I spent the afternoon in the nursery. Thank God for little children. Their love was genuine.

Was it gratitude or joy that set my heart beating wildly when George walked in on us? He lifted in turn, each of the children, hugging and kissing them, and then, 'Could I have a word with you, Sophy . . . in private?'

I led the way down to my room. Quietly closing the door, he faced me, holding out a piece of paper. 'Read this,' he said in a voice so tense with emotion, that I looked at him in alarm. 'Go on. Read it,' he urged. 'I found it among Mama's papers.'

It was some form of document, old and faded. I took it over to the window that I might decipher the writing. It was a marriage certificate, stating that a marriage had been solemnized between one William Cavendish, bachelor, and Lucy Ashby, spinster.

I looked up at George, a new lightness flooding my heart, joy for both of us, knowing that I was a child of a loving marriage and that Lady Perriman had been no frail light o'love. He must have read my mind for he merely indicated. 'Read the other side.' The ink had faded, but there, in Lady Perriman's neat handwriting were the tragic words, 'Widowed one week later, when my beloved William was killed in a duel, by my brother, Martyn. May God forgive him, for I shall never be able to do so.'

Now, for the first time since George's homecoming, my tears began to flow. He put a comforting arm around me, holding me close until the first paroxysm of grief had passed.

'Do you . . . do you think, she would ever have told me?'

There was a touch of irony in his voice as he answered, 'When we had gone to her, asking her blessing on our marriage, she would have been compelled to tell us would she not? Thank God we were spared that. I can only presume that your birth was kept secret at the insistence of her family . . . probably the marriage with my father having already been arranged. Poor Mama . . . how desperate she must have been . . . hiding you until . . . little knowing the misfortune that had befallen you . . . '

Listening to him seeing the picture he presented, I was totally unprepared for the break in his voice and his agonised cry, 'Oh, God help me, Sophy. How am I going to reconcile myself to loving you as a sister, when I so adore you . . . worship you . . . '

'Hush, George, hush.' Without thinking, I went over to him, going down on my knees, resting my head against him, 'It is wrong, now, to think or talk that way.'

He lifted my chin, forcing my eyes to meet his. ' . . . and you would have let me think you had been false to our love rather than betray my . . . our mother.' Then his mouth was on mine; his kiss hard and long before releasing me and helping me regain my feet, remarking with bitterness, 'You need have no further fear, little sister.'

I could only whisper, 'I will leave here as soon as possible.'

' . . . To marry another man? The final thrust in the wound. Oh God! Oh God!' He suddenly braced himself. 'Forgive me Sophy. I do wish you happiness in your marriage. Such sweetness as yours was never intended to be wasted on spinsterhood. As soon as my immediate affairs are settled, I will visit our Ashby relations and endeavour to find some information about your father. As for myself, I shall follow my father's example. Live life to the full in London.

I understand now. He never had my mother's love. He was lonely as I shall be for the rest of my life.'

I looked at him reproachfully. 'Would you waste your life? What about all the plans you had for Perriman? No, you will find some wonderful girl to be your help-mate . . . ' When he did not reply, I continued, 'I should indeed be most grateful to know more about my father.'

Gently he waived my thanks aside and was about to leave when he suddenly turned, 'I almost forgot to tell you. Barbara and I are driving over to Mary's in time for dinner and staying the night. As a newly-wed wife, she can't wait to show me her new possessions.'

He must have seen the surprise in my eyes for he quickly went on, 'I know Sophy, I know. 'Tis mighty uncivil not to have included you in the invitation . . . '

'I am not concerned. As Aunt Lucy's

241

ward, I was not always invited with the others . . . '

'Maybe not, but now you are Mary's half-sister . . . ' ' . . . To her shame and embarrassment, yes. I can understand her attitude. I shall be happier here . . . '

He gave a mirthless laugh. 'At the earliest opportunity when they are all together, I shall bring out this piece of paper. Last night, they poured scorn on Mama, as if she was a fallen woman. Tonight, they will learn otherwise.' Abruptly, he left the room.

Not for worlds, would I have let him know, how deep the hurt had gone. It was obvious they were intent on rejecting me. They wanted me to leave Perriman Court . . . to go right out of their lives. I was the living symbol of some ghastly error in their mother's life.

Barbara came bouncing into my room. 'Have you heard George and I are going to Mary's . . . ?'

'Yes. George told me but a few

moments ago . . . '

'Did he tell you why Mary had invited him!'

'To see her new home . . . her splendid new furniture . . . '

'Is that what he told you? Men are deceivers ever! No, it's Isobel Saunders! You know, she was crazy about him before he went away . . . and he over her. Well, she's just back from her finishing-school and when Mary remarked her family was her nearest neighbour, George said he must come over and renew the acquaintance. So . . . Mary is inviting her over tonight . . . and knowing Isobel . . . no matter what engagements she has . . . she'll drop them all and come running to be in George's company again.'

I knew it was only too true. Not only was Isobel crazy over George but so were her parents and now that he was Lord Perriman . . . it would be a wonderful match.

But I told myself proudly. I am Sophia Cavendish. Sophia Cavendish.

I whispered the name to myself, over and over again, until the name of Isobel Saunders crept into my mind again. In that moment I felt I hated everybody but none more than Isobel. George belonged to me . . . and then I threw myself on the bed and wept.

8

I had dinner in my room that night, solitary and lonely. My mind was so pestered, I could not settle down to my novel nor my embroidery. I tried walking in the garden but the figures of George and Isobel would keep intruding and walking alongside me. I could hear their conversation; George at his most charming, talking sweet nonsense. Would he dare to put his arm around her waist? Or kiss her? I could well imagine her Mama giving her advice . . . advice on how to encourage him . . . to let him know his advances would be most welcome.

I fled from them, back to my room, deciding, having visited Martha, I would have an early night. Dear Martha. I felt certain George's homecoming had brought about some improvement. She looked brighter . . . happier . . . she was using her mouth more, trying to talk. Every night, I prayed for the miracle, that she might recover her speech and answer the questions my aching heart and bemused mind stirred with each new day.

I must have fallen asleep almost as soon as I put my head on the pillow, for some time in the night, I awoke feeling quite fresh. It was still dark and not a sound to be heard, that telling me, the hour must be very early, otherwise the servants would be about. Yet something had disturbed me. I listened intently. Dead silence but there was something . . . What could I smell? Smoke? Instantly, I was out of bed, peering through the window and there to my horror, were great clouds of smoke coming from the stables. Thrusting my feet into slippers and grabbing a wrap, I ran down the stairs shouting loudly. 'Fire! Fire in the stables! Everybody get up . . . '

The stables were some distance from the house but it took me but a few minutes, for never did I run so quickly. How the stable boys and grooms could still be asleep mystified me, for the horses could be heard whinnying and stamping about. There was a bell in the yard, which I pulled on furiously, but there was no response from the men's sleeping quarters? Had they been suffocated? As quick as my trembling fingers would allow, I drew back one bolt after another of the horse-boxes giving each animal a comforting pat and a soothing word as he dashed out of the smoke into the cobbled yard.

Now the household staff had joined me and having located the source of the fire had quickly formed a chain of water-buckets from the nearest ornamental pool. Mercifully, the flames were confined to the loose box where fodder was stacked, which had been carelessly or deliberately set on fire.

As soon as the smoke had cleared sufficient to allow entry, search was made for the stablemen but there was no sign of a single man, dead or alive.

Where were they, I demanded, it was their job to guard the horses.

The butler, Hadgett, supplied the answer. 'Down at the Honeysuckle Bee, I expect. Drinking and wenching. They knew his Lordship was away overnight and that they wouldn't be called upon . . . so they made the most of the opportunity. Some of the footmen also took French leave, but they'll all be back in time for their morning duties . . . '

' . . . but the horses might have been burned to death! The fire might have reached the house if I hadn't happened to wake up . . . '

'His Lordship won't know how to thank you, Miss Sophia.' It was Mr. Long. 'You were very brave. The horses might have stampeded . . . trampled on you . . . but see, you are wet through. Come back to the house, child. There is no danger now.'

I was loth to leave the animals for the smoke was still dense, so opening the yard door, I led them into the paddock where they could graze and recover their sense of security.

'Miss Sophia . . . you'll catch your death of cold.' Again it was Mr. Long, so anxious for my well-being. As we walked back to the house, I asked, 'Who do you think started the fire, sir. Not one of our men, surely, for they seem contented enough?'

'No, 'twill be one of these roaming parties of reformers, marching down to London, setting fire to houses and farms as they go . . . '

'We saw some of them when we went to London. They threw stones at the carriage and shouted coarse words . . . '

'Yes, they are very dangerous men to encounter . . . '

'Are they not also hungry . . . and angry men? Angry because their masters will not pay sufficient wages for them to maintain their families free from hunger?'

He looked at me strangely. 'You talk, Miss Sophia as though you favour Reform . . . '

'I favour treating men like human beings. It is dreadful to think that they are less cared for than our horses . . . '

Dawn was now breaking and reaching Mr. Long's apartments, we found Mrs. Long waiting with hot drinks. Plying us with questions, she fussed over me, taking me to her bedroom and supplying me with dry slippers and a wrap. It was then, I heard the commotion out on the terrace . . . shouting and yelling. Heedless of Mrs. Long's apprehension, I followed her husband. There, a number of our lackeys were dragging along a wretched specimen of a man, almost in rags, seemingly unable to walk, yet being subjected to blows from first one and then another of his captors.

'We caught him in the orchard, sir! He's one of them, right enough. Shall we send for the militia, sir?'

Mr. Long eyed the man sternly. 'What do you know about this business? Did you set the stables on fire?'

'No, sir, no. I swear it . . . '

'Then what were you doing in the orchard?'

'I . . . I . . . I was looking for . . . for any fallen fruit . . . '

A roar of ribald laughter went up from the men around him. 'A likely tale . . . '

'I haven't had anything to eat since I hurt my leg two days ago . . . and couldn't keep up with the others on the march . . . '

'Ah, then, you do admit you are with one of these gangs of desperadoes . . . so called Reformers . . . '

'I was, sir . . . until they left me behind. Then I lost my way . . . '

'Then who do you suppose set fire to our stables?'

'I couldn't say, sir . . . There are other protests marching down . . . '

'He's lying, sir.' It was the butler again, a pompous individual who considered himself the virtual head of Perriman Court. 'I could put him in one of the cellars until his Lordship returns, in case he wishes to question him. Or should we waste no time and send for the Militia now?'

'Please . . . no . . . Don't send for the Militia. They'll hang me . . . I've got a wife and bairns back home . . .'

'You should have thought of that before. Have I your permission, sir, to take him below?'

Mr. Long hesitated giving me a chance to break in. 'You'll take him nowhere, until you have given him some food. Get some game pie and beer . . .'

Hadgett regarded me haughtily but snapping his fingers in the direction of a flunkey, ordered the food to be brought.

I had never seen a grown man so ravenous for food. It was revolting the way he ate that pie. I turned away and went up to my room but not to sleep or dress. Going to Aunt Lucy's medicine cupboard, I took out a jar of ointment and some strips of linen and finding Hadgett, asked what he had done with the man.

With his fingers, he indicated below. 'That will give him a chance to cool his heels, Miss Sophia, before they string him up. We've sent word to His Lordship so he should be here before noon.'

As soon as he was out of sight, I slipped down to the cellars. I shivered in the unnatural chill and gloom, for I was still wearing only my nightrobe and a wrap. Where had they put the poor wretch? Then I noticed the small cupboard securely bolted. Pulling back the fastener, I helped the man to crawl from his cramped prison. 'Now let me have a look at that leg.'

The poor creature demurred ' . . . my legs aren't fit for the likes of you to touch . . . '

I did indeed wish I had brought soap and water but there was no time to be lost. It was a long deep cut . . . already festering. As best I could, I wiped away some of the dirt and then applied the ointment finally binding it with the linen.

He looked at me with gratitude. 'I don't know why you're doing this, miss . . . '

'Because you've a wife waiting for your return . . . '

'But how . . . ?'

I pushed a parcel into his hands. 'It's only bread and cheese . . . but here is some money . . . ' I tried to appear stern. 'Mind you, if I thought for one minute, you had anything to do with the firing of the stables, I would be the first to send for the Militia . . . '

'I swear it, miss, I know nothing about it . . . '

'Working for reform is one thing; but the burning and looting of property is wicked and evil . . . '

'I'll go back, miss . . . and bless you . . . '

He followed me up the steps where we emerged on to the back of the house. 'Now go straight down the path. If you meet anyone, touch your cap to them. If they speak, tell them you're on an urgent message into the village . . . and God go with you.'

I hurried away. I found his thanks embarrassing, for I knew that I should have to answer for my rash behaviour.

I heard George's carriage dash up to the entrance and looking from my window, saw that Mary and her husband had accompanied him and Barbara. Obviously, I told myself wryly, Mary didn't intend to miss any excitement.

They had been back about half an hour when a maid came to my room asking would I go down to the library. I took a deep breath as I entered and found myself facing a bewildered looking George together with his scornful sisters and brother-in-law.

Poor George. He hardly knew where to begin, then hesitantly, 'Sophy . . . you knew that a prisoner was captured this morning . . . '

I had a sudden impulse to laugh. He made it sound as though an important prisoner of war had escaped.

'Why, yes, sir . . . '

'He was made secure in one of the cellars . . . '

'So I was told, sir . . . '

' . . . and I am told that you were full of concern for him . . . '

'He was hungry and he had been hurt . . . '

' . . . and you gave him food . . . '

'It was the least I could do . . . '

'Did you know that he has escaped?'

'For God's sake, George, stop playing with words. Of course, she knows. She set him free.'

Henry's voice was dictatorial and insolent, 'Didn't you Miss?'

I faced him, equally insolent. 'I did. He deserved another chance . . . '

'Another chance? To do what? Burn down more houses? Perhaps my house . . . ?'

'Sophia, you are totally untrustworthy. You are not fit to be left in charge of Perriman.' Now Mary was giving vent to her feelings. 'My little brother and sisters could have been burnt to death in their beds . . . hob-nobbing with such scum . . . '

I looked at George, 'Have I your permission to retire, sir?'

He gave a sigh of resignation. 'Yes. There is nothing more you can tell us. The fellow will be far away by now . . . '

I favoured them all with an impish grin, 'I do hope so, I really do.'

★ ★ ★

Being anxious to avoid the rest of the family, I decided to visit the horses after their last night's ordeal. Some of them were back in their boxes but others were grazing in the paddock. On my approach, the stable-hands looked away, sheepish and ashamed. I had been there but a few minutes, when George came striding across the yard, 'I've been searching for you everywhere, Sophy . . . but please leave us for a few minutes.'

I would dearly have loved to have

heard him dressing down those men, most probably using his most shocking army language but obediently, I strolled into the paddock, nuzzling up to first one animal and then another.

When George joined me, he put an arm around my shoulder and there was a break in his voice as he asked, 'Sophy, can you ever forgive me? I did not know that we have you to thank for saving the horses . . . and perhaps the Court itself . . . and I let them insult you . . . '

'La George, it is of no account. It amused me to see their angry faces . . . '

'But you took such risks. Mr. Long could not praise you enough for your courage and resourcefulness . . . '

He took my hand and drew me down on to the soft, springy, turf, so that our backs rested against a huge walnut tree, 'Last night, I showed them the marriage certificate . . . '

'And are they now satisfied as to their mother's worthiness?'

'They were considerably abashed, speculating as to who Mr. Cavendish might have been.'

'Only Martha can tell us that,' I sighed. 'Dear God, that she might tell us soon . . . then I could leave . . . '

'Are you in such a hurry to leave me, Sophy? You are still intent on marrying Mr. Masters?'

'As my legal guardian, he intends asking you for my hand . . . '

He groaned, 'And I am expected to give away the only girl I ever wanted . . . '

'What about Isobel?' I asked mischievously.

'Isobel? Oh that stupid girl at Mary's dinner party. What about her?'

'Would she not make you an excellent wife?'

'I have no intention to marry . . . '

'La, George, I cannot visualise you as a crusty bachelor . . . '

Abruptly changing the subject, he asked, 'Why did you let that fellow go this morning? Not that I am really

blaming you . . . you had the right
. . . but why, when such a fellow is
a danger to the community?'

'As an individual, he is no danger.
It is only when many of his kind
get together, full of bitterness and
resentment about their unhappy lot.
Reform, there must be. Until there is,
there will be constant trouble up and
down the country.'

His eyes were wide with surprise.
'You speak as a rabid Reformist,
yourself . . . '

'I have, on several occasions discussed
the subject with Mr. Masters . . . '

'I might have guessed the fellow
would have such tendencies . . . '

'Your father, too, had such tendencies
. . . and although he may not be aware
of it, his son thinks in a similar vein,
when he talks of the improvements he
is going to bring about for Perriman
tenants and workers . . . '

'Sophy . . . you are still as big a
minx as ever. You know,' he went
on, 'you are not a bit like Mama,

neither in looks nor ways. She was so quiet and withdrawn, while you are free and outspoken . . . so much more alive . . . '

'Perhaps her heart died when my father was killed . . . '

' . . . even as mine died, when I found I could not marry you.'

★ ★ ★

Dinner passed off without anything untoward being said. George seemed relieved to have male company in the person of his brother-in-law, Henry, the chief topic of conversation being last night's fire but I knew that before the evening was over, Mary or Barbara would bring up the subject of the marriage certificate. It was Barbara who broached it . . . perhaps she only meant it as a joke but her manner angered me. 'Ah, Lady Stainton . . . may I present you to my half-sister, Miss Sophia Cavendish. Miss Cavendish, my sister, Mary, Lady Stainton.'

'I still maintain' broke in Mary, 'that Mama did Papa a grave injustice in not telling him of her previous marriage and the child . . . '

'But can't you see, Mary,' protested her brother, 'that she must have been under great pressure from her family and not to speak a word of the business. She was sent away until the child had been born and fostered out, while they smugly arranged a marriage with the Perriman family . . . a disgusting, heartless procedure . . . '

Barbara's nose was twitching with disdain, 'Well, I think Martha was a wicked woman to help Mama in her deceit . . . '

'You only say that because Martha had more occasion to spank you than the rest of us,' was George's dry comment, 'But if we are honest, we must admit she did it for the best. She loved Mama. I knew she was unhappy. Often when she took me on her knee, she would cry and then Martha would comfort her, 'Don't cry,

Miss Lucy. Someday . . . ' I used to wonder about that 'someday'. Now I know. It was the red-letter day when she would once again hold her little daughter in her arms.'

He looked at me with a smile. 'How I remember that day! How I thank God you came when you did. Otherwise . . . '

Neither Barbara nor Mary were in the mood for reminiscing. 'What a horrible scandal there will be,' moaned Mary.

There was impatience in George's voice. 'There will be no scandal if we keep the matter secret among ourselves. If ever this workhouse creature comes here again, trying to blackmail either me or Sophy, I shall know how to deal with her. Blackmail is a serious crime.

'But there's nothing to stop her from spreading the story around,' expostulated Barbara. 'Oh, Sophy won't mind,' she went on sarcastically, 'because the story is to her betterment, while we must bear the brunt of the disgrace . . . '

'For the love of God, try to forget your stupid pride and show a little sympathy for Mama.' George glared first at Mary and then at Barbara. 'I wonder how either of you would have acted under similar circumstances. As for condemning Martha, thank God, Mama had one friend.'

9

Dawn was breaking, and as yet, sleep had eluded me. Over and over again, I recounted to myself all that had happened . . . all that had been said, since George came home . . . since the clouds of mistrust and suspicion had descended on Perriman Court.

But oh, thank God, for that one golden shaft of light; that scrap of faded yellow paper . . . my mother's marriage certificate. Now I knew my real name. 'Sophia Cavendish,' I whispered. 'Sophia Cavendish.'

As I lay in the faint light, listening to the rising wind, I was aware of my thankfulness there had been no wind the night before, otherwise the flames might have reached the Court. I shuddered at the thought of the beautiful house reduced to a pile of stones.

But now, I must begin to think of the future. I had promised to write to Julian as soon as George came home but somehow, I felt an odd reluctance, as though I needed more time to compose my bemused mind . . . perhaps even to get away from Perriman before I wrote. I must leave Perriman soon, if only for George's sake. His agonised face rose before me . . . the agony of a useless, frustrated love and it was in that moment, the realisation came. I was still in love with my half-brother.

In that moment, I knew that I could never marry Julian or any other man.

The wind was now whipping itself into a fury, the windows rattled as if a giant was shaking them while the drapes were billowing out into the room like a ship in full sail.

Getting out of bed to close the casements, I was amazed to see tall, strong trees bending almost double in the force of the gale, only to recover and lift themselves upright again, ready to meet the next onslaught.

Back in the comfort of my bed, I sat hugging my knees. I would be like one of those trees. No matter how much I was bludgeoned by the turn of events, I would face up to the world. I was Sophia Cavendish. I found myself wondering about my father. He must have been a fine, splendid man, for a sweet lady like Lady Perriman to have loved him enough, to elope, to have risked the anger of her parents. What she must have suffered both before and after I was born and yet, I could see that it had been most unfair on Lord Perriman to be married to a wife who was incapable of loving him. That I told myself angrily, was the fault of her parents.

A sudden, cracking, tearing, splitting noise rent the morning air. Somewhere, not too far away, a noble tree had fallen victim to the tempest. Now the wind had reached hurricane force, whistling round the house, as though searching for a weakness, so as to wreak its devilish mischief.

I suddenly thought of Martha. No-one could sleep through this diabolical row and if the opiate had lost its effect . . .

Wearing only a light wrapper over my nightrobe, I hurried to her room.

She was indeed awake, her eyes wide open, giving a sign of recognition. The night nurse rose to her feet. 'She's been awake quite a while now, Miss Sophia . . . and trying to talk . . . saying your name.'

I took the bedside chair she had just vacated. 'With such a rough night, I doubt if any of us have had much sleep. A dish of tea, would, I am sure be much appreciated by all of us.'

As soon as she had gone, I slipped on my knees, 'Martha,' I said softly.

There seemed an endless wait, then hardly able to believe my ears, she spoke, 'Sophy . . . George . . . home . . .'

'Yes, dear Martha . . .'

'You marry . . . him . . . not . . . not . . . what . . . what she said, you . . . marry . . . George.'

It was a miracle that her voice had come back, but dear God, was her mind wandering?

'Not what she said?' I prompted slowly.

There was a long pause, then slowly shaking her head. 'You . . . not . . . not . . . Miss Lucy's baby . . . '

For an instant it seemed that a flashing red light seared my eyes and understanding, so that I had to fight to keep control of my senses. There was more that I must know.

She was speaking again but so low that I had to bend over to her lips.

'Her . . . her baby . . . was . . . was dead . . . when . . . when I gave it to . . . to . . . '

'To the Bartons',' I asked sharply.

She nodded.

So I was not Lady Perriman's child. I was not Sophia Cavendish. In that instant, all hope of claiming to be of decent birth died within me. I tried to repress my anguish but my voice would not be denied and I heard myself almost shouting, 'Then who am I? Tell me, Martha, who am I?' The cry came from the very depths of my soul.

She looked up at me, shaking her head, 'I . . . I . . . don't know, lovey . . . I . . . I . . . don't know.'

An overwhelming wave of resentment engulfed me. For an instant, I felt I wanted to shake her, if by doing so, she could be made to tell me a straightforward, coherent story. Instead, I asked slowly, 'Why then, was I brought here?'

Her mouth quivered pitifully, as though trying to keep back the tears.

'Never . . . never . . . told . . . Miss Lucy. She . . . she wanted baby . . . wanted . . . to go, . . . go back . . . to . . . get . . . baby.'

I tried to piece together the chain of events.

'You and Lady Perriman went to

Curton . . . to get the child . . . now nine years old?'

A nod was her only reply.

I put my arm around her poor thin shoulders and stressing every word, I asked, 'Why didn't you tell Lady Perriman her baby was dead?'

She shook her head before attempting to speak. 'She . . . she was ill. So . . . so very ill . . . her poor head . . . she would cry . . . every day . . . '

'Listen, Martha. When you found Mrs. Barton had died and that Mr. Barton had put a baby into the workhouse, you knew that child was not Lady Perriman's. Yet you let her think it was. Why, Martha, why?'

To my amazement, a smile illuminated her face. 'It made her happy . . . so very . . . very . . . happy. You . . . made . . . her . . . happy . . . '

I knew the rest of the story. I didn't need Martha to tell me any more. She knew no more. I was back where I had started. A workhouse bastard. Parentage unknown. In my agony of mind, I prayed aloud, 'Oh, God, who am I? Tell me. Who am I?'

I felt the movement of Martha's fingers, touching my hand. Lovingly, I enclosed them between my palms.

'Sorry . . . so sorry . . . little Sophy. She . . . loved you. I . . . I . . . loved you . . . you . . . made us . . . both . . . so . . . so . . . happy . . . '

She gave a sigh as though of contentment and even as I watched, I saw the change come over her.

'Martha . . . don't leave me . . . I need you . . . ' My sobbing brought servants running into the room and I allowed them to lift and lead me away.

At the doorway, I turned, but already the sheet had been lifted over Martha's face.

Feeling that George would wish to be told immediately, but more because I felt the need of someone to share my grief, I hastily sent a message to his room.

As I awaited him, I tried to come to

some decision as to whether I should tell him of Martha's disclosures. When he entered the room, should I cry out, 'George, my dearest, I am not your sister ... I am not your mother's child ... I can fulfil my promise to marry you after all, for I do love you so very much ...' No, I could not do that. My pride would not allow it. In the first place, why give the arrogant Perriman girls the satisfaction of knowing that I truly was a nameless bastard? And secondly, was there not the danger of even George thinking that I was anxious to be Lady Perriman? Yet deep down, I knew that I had but to tell him and he would insist on our marriage. But I was not a fit person to be Lady Perriman. To marry him would mean a life of opposition and ostracism for both of us from the rest of the family.

Mercifully, I was saved from any further wallowing in my misery by his arrival. He took one look at me and then instructed a maid to bring the doctor as quickly as possible.

'It has all been too much for you Sophy.' He turned to Dorcas. 'Get Miss Sophia into bed. Can't you see she's almost in a state of collapse?' I made no protest. The quick succession of events had indeed so bewildered me, that I felt totally incapable of clear thinking. I made no demur about the opiate. I just wanted to sleep and sleep . . . to forget.

I slept late into the afternoon. For a while, I lay there, marshalling my thoughts. Martha was dead. I was not Lady Perriman's child. I could not marry Julian Masters for I was still in love with George. The sooner I was away from Perriman Court, the better for all concerned.

In answer to my bell, Dorcas came hurrying in, drawing back the drapes, letting in the mellow afternoon sunshine.

'Thank goodness, Miss Sophia, you're looking better now. What a fright you gave us all! You looked like a corpse yourself. Lord Perriman was frantic about you. Now, shall I bring you a dish of tea?'

'There's nothing I should like better . . . and my writing desk, please.'

I must write to Julian. I told him of everything that had happened. Then I tore it up. I still felt so bruised and shaken, that as yet I couldn't even contemplate his knowing. I wanted to be alone; to find myself; to get back my self-respect, for now I felt as though I was grovelling in the dirty slime of the dried-up canal at Curton, the playground of my childhood. I would go to Curton. I would search out this Mr. Barton. I wanted to know the truth. Why hadn't he reported the baby's death? I would make him tell me the truth about everything . . . and most important of all, he should tell me how I came to be in his home. Another foster child, no doubt. But whose child? Who was my mother . . . and my father?

I began to feel better. The prospect

of doing something active, acted as an elixir. Mr. Stevens was coming today. I would ask him about my money. He had already given me an advance and I was going to need it all for another idea had come into my mind. It wasn't exactly new but a notion I had been contemplating over the years since I had become aware of the unfairness of life. I would start a home for unwanted children; a home where they could be brought up in love and kindness. How far would £200 a year go? In one bad moment, I had thought of flinging it back at the Perrimans' but then my low birth urged me to take it, being legally mine. I began to feel excited about travelling alone. I would have to go by mail coach. Would I ever come back to Perriman Court? What about my clothes?

I was debating with myself as to whether I should join the family for dinner. They would not want my company of that I was sure but why should I stay up here now that I had got rid of my mops. There was a tap on the door and at my answering call, George came in.

He seated himself alongside my bed. 'I heard you were awake at last. How are you feeling? It was terrible that you should have been alone with Martha . . . at the last.'

'Her passing was very peaceful, but now that she has gone, I feel such a desolation . . . '

'Yes, . . . she was like a second mother to us, but perhaps it is a blessing really. Poor Martha, lying there, week after week, never speaking . . . '

I had a sudden impulse to cry out, 'But she did speak! She told me . . . ' and then my courage failed and George was persuading me to come down to dinner that evening.

'Henry has arrived, so Mary will be too engrossed with him to make more snide remarks.'

'I care not what she says and Barbara is but a child . . . ' There was an air of recklessness in my voice. Should I tell him of my plans? Instead, I asked, 'Has Mr. Stevens arrived?'

'Indeed, yes. I have been closeted with him all the afternoon. He will also be dining with us.'

'Then perhaps you would arrange that I could have a few words with him.'

'About your money? He told me of the dowry and legacy. I am glad about that Sophy . . . '

'At least it frees you, of any dutiful obligation . . . '

'What will you do Sophy? You know you can stay here. After all, it is your home . . . '

Dear, dear George. If only I could tell him but I shook my head. 'No George, no. I must leave as soon as possible.'

'But where will you go? £200 is not much for you . . . not for the mode of living you are accustomed to . . . '

I felt an impish notion to tease him as I did in our happy childhood days. 'I'm seriously thinking of going on the stage. Ever since Lord Perriman took us to the theatre. I've been entranced with the possibility.'

'Good God, Sophy no! You can have no notion of the vulgar type of woman . . . I could almost say immoral woman and the lustful type of man that pursues her . . . '

'Don't look so horrified, George. I can sing . . . I can dance . . . just think how proud you would be to visit the theatre and say, 'I know that actress. She is my . . . '

'The devil I would! I would disown you . . . '

'Fie on you, George for your prigishness. Do you know any actresses? No? Then how can you make such cutting remarks? From what I have heard, they are much sought after by the gentry . . . '

'For passing amusement only . . . or to be their mistresses . . . '

'Then a curse on all such men who seek out women possessed of most charm, only to discard them. I will be the most perverse of actresses . . . lead them on and then laugh in their faces and watch them crawl away . . . oh so abject . . . '

'Don't play with fire, Sophy. You are so sweet and innocent of the world . . . '

As he rose, he kissed me gently . . . a brotherly peck . . . and then silently he left the room. I wanted to call after him, to bid him come back and take me in his arms and kiss me as he had done that morning by the side of the lake. Again, I realised the wicked wanton within me, burying my head in my hands, as though to hide the shame from myself. I suddenly recalled last night's gale but looking out of the window, I could not see one tell-tale twig or branch marring the sweeping lawns. The Perriman gardeners took a pride in their work. They would have been at work all day, so that all disorder should be swept away. As I gazed, my determination strengthened. Just now, my life appeared to be chaotic and bewildered, but somehow, even at the risk of discovering something I did not like, I was determined to find the secret of my birth.

10

There was a letter from Julian the next morning. My first impulse was to throw it on the fire unread, but then my contrary heart stepped in and I pushed it deep into my reticule to be read after the funeral.

George had given orders that all the household staff who could be spared, together with the estate workers should attend Martha's funeral service. He and I, however, were the only mourners to accompany Mr. Long to the graveside in Perriman village churchyard.

Poor Martha. No family or relatives of her own to bid her farewell. The Perrimans had been her life. The Perriman children had been her children. I had been but the pawn in her game of restoring her mistress's happiness. Yet I had loved Martha. Perhaps it was the inborn recognition that we both belonged to the seamy side of life.

A farm wagon had conveyed the coffin, we following in a Perriman coach, with neither of us speaking a word; a silence we maintained at the graveside, but on the return journey, George was anxious to talk.

'Sophy . . . I know these last few days . . . since I came home . . . must have been torment for you. I am ashamed of the way my sisters have behaved . . . 'tis more than I can understand.'

'Events have not proved very happy for you either,' I began, in an attempt to speak sympathetically. 'I'm truly sorry you have had such a wretched home-coming . . . '

'Where do we begin to affix the blame?' George's voice was morose. 'The Bible speaks true. The sins of the fathers unto the third and fourth generation. Oh, Sophy . . . Sophy, I cannot think of you as my half-sister. My love for you is as deep as ever. With every passing day, I feel the need for you more and more . . . '

'Don't George. Don't.' The tears came into my eyes. It would be so easy to tell him now but I had already caused too much chaos in this family that had done so much for me. 'All the more reason why I should leave without any further delay . . . '

We were still arguing round the point when we drove up to the main entrance steps; George doing his utmost to persuade me to stay, if only for the sake of the children . . . I remaining stubborn and adamant.

Back in my room, I took out Julian's letter.

My Dearest Sophia,

This is but a short note to say I am journeying over to France and will be out of the country for a few days.

By the time I return to London, I pray your letter will be awaiting me, telling of Lord Perriman's home-coming and bidding me speed up to Yorkshire.

I am beginning to grow impatient.
Till we meet, Julian.

Farewell, my dear Julian for now I know I can never marry you. Thank you for everything. You were a dear friend in my darkest hour. I shall always be grateful.

Sooner or later, I must answer this letter. He deserved an explanation, but just what . . . or how much I should tell him, I was not sure, but now I knew it was more urgent than ever I should leave the Court. Julian was growing impatient. Somehow I felt, that when he found no letter on his return, he would come up to Yorkshire poste-haste. Should I warn George of the possibility, or let matters take their course? Pray God, I was away before he arrived.

I tried to organise a plan. I would go to London. I would ask Mr. Stevens to find me a small house, in keeping with my income. When I had talked to George of going on the stage, it was not just a teasing jest, for I really had given much thought to the matter. Then I realised how easily Julian could seek me out . . . bombard me with more proposals of marriage. No, I would not go to London. There would be theatres in Manchester . . . perhaps I could find employment there . . . I had never heard of Julian visiting Lancashire . . . and provincial actresses caused no stir . . . but first of all I had some business to settle at near-by Curton, that ugly little town, where I had spent my early life . . . in the workhouse. Whatever shape my other plans might take, I was still determined to solve the riddle of my parentage.

I was awake early the next morning for I wished to be away before anyone was about. I had worked well into the early hours packing all my belongings. I had written a brief note to George telling him of my intentions and that when I had a permanent address, I would be grateful if my boxes could be sent on to me.

I had also written to Julian, leaving it to be handed to him when he came to Perriman. It had been a difficult letter to write. I hated hurting him. He was so kind himself. I did not tell him of Martha's last words. Let him go on thinking I was George's half sister, but I had to tell him that I did not love him sufficiently to become his wife. He deserved a wholehearted love.

I dare not go and kiss little Charles goodbye; to have done so, would have confused all my resolutions. Instead, picking up the small bag, containing my immediate necessities, I hurried in the direction of the stables.

There, the grooms and stable-boys were already at work. They stared at me in surprise as I approached the head groom and asked if I might have a horse harnessed to a dog cart and a groom to take me to the market square, when a voice behind me queried, 'You going away, Miss Sophia?'

It was Mr. Long.

'But for a few days,' I stammered, 'I

came looking for a conveyance as far as the mail-coach . . . '

'Are you running away, Sophia?' he asked softly.

'Not exactly . . . Lord Perriman knows I am making this journey but I prefer to be gone before he comes down to breakfast.'

'But you are not accustomed to travelling alone. You do not know the risks . . . '

'Sir! I really wish to be away.' My interruption was brusque, almost rude, but the good gentleman now saw my urgency.

'Well, then, Miss Sophia, we'll be on our way. I had just come to order my gig to take me down to the church. I shall enjoy your company,' and with little to-do, there I was, seated beside him, trotting along the beech-grove.

For a while, neither of us spoke. I was far from feeling happy or excited, I was too miserable at the prospect of never seeing Perriman again. As we drove along the narrow, dusty road, the hedgerows and undulating meadows presenting a picture of beauty that I knew would be imprinted on my mind forever I had a sudden impulse to ask Mr. Long to stop . . . to allow me to go back, but the mood passed. I must not weaken.

As though aware of my thoughts, Mr. Long's voice cut in, 'Are you sure you are doing the right thing, Miss Sophia? This Mr. Masters, did you not promise to marry him, and I am told by Mr. Stevens he is due here any day now.'

'That is one of the reasons why I am going away. I find now that I can not marry him.'

'May I, as a parson and a friend be impertinent and ask the reason?'

'For the best reason in the world, sir. I do not love him. My decision is for his sake as much as my own.'

'You are very young and inexperienced, Sophia — I wonder what love means to you.'

I was silent. How could I tell the

reverend man of my longing for one man . . . one man only? How could I begin to explain the havoc within me when that man took me in his arms and our lips met? How could I explain that though a man was good and kind and honourable, I still had no wish to marry him?

'Mr. Masters will go far,' I began feebly. 'He is very ambitious and with the right helpmate . . . ' My voice died away for I felt a sudden desire to confide in someone and who better than a clergyman? 'Mr. Long, I would like to tell you something. Then perhaps you will understand why I cannot marry Mr. Masters. It . . . it was a confidence, the late Lord Perriman gave me. Now . . . now that . . . he is no longer here. I am sure he would not mind me repeating it.'

Mr. Long's eyebrows went up, 'The late Lord Perriman spoke in confidence with you?'

'Yes, . . . concerning his marriage with Lady Perriman. He was deeply in love with her . . . but his love was unrequited. Why, he did not know, but since we have seen that marriage certificate, we know only too well. His last words to me on that occasion were that when I married, I must be sure that I loved the man . . . and that he loved me . . . regardless of his wealth or position . . . or even his poverty. Now do you understand, sir?'

For a moment he did not reply. He seemed to be turning some matter over in his mind, then very quietly, 'Indeed I do Miss Sophia . . . but, you will come back to us I am sure. In the meantime, I cannot bear to think of you going out into the world alone. You do not know the risks . . . '

'I am not afraid. I shall endeavour to find some kind of employment. I cannot face a lifetime of futile living . . . '

He pursued the question no further, talking of other matters as we drove along. Dear, kind Mr. Long. He insisted on staying with me until the mail coach arrived, protesting that

George would be most put out that I had not availed myself of a Perriman carriage.

Then with his repeated wishes for a safe journey and my speedy return ringing in my ears, the coach rumbled on, as I tried to edge myself comfortably between two elderly ladies who seemed to regard me as an object of curiosity, so young to be travelling alone.

11

I soon came to the realisation that I did not like travelling by mail-coach. The springs were so inadequate that whenever we passed over a hole in the road, we were tossed and jerked in the most painful manner and the roads appeared to be in a really lamentable condition. The leather upholstery of the coach was torn and dirty and we had not gone many miles before the atmosphere became so heavy and fuggy that I timidly asked the passenger nearest the window if we might have a little fresh air, only to be greeted by hostile stares and acid comments that the air at this time of year was positively menacing but that the young had no consideration for their elders.

Neither had I liked my bed at the coaching-inn where we had stayed overnight and I was glad to be on my way the next morning by the first available coach.

Ruefully, I told myself, I must become accustomed to this mode of travel and having obtained a window-seat, I determined to be more tolerant. The recollection of having journeyed on this road before, even though it was in the opposite direction, brought back nostalgic memories.

What an odd, ugly little brat I must have appeared on that occasion . . . thin, pale, shorn as close as a sheep at shearing-time. I recalled my first impression of the Perriman coach. I could actually smell its tangy cleanliness and feel its comfort. Once again, Martha was handing pastries to me from the luncheon basket; I could see Lady Perriman sitting opposite, smiling indulgently. Poor dear Aunt Lucy; she thought she was smiling at her own little daughter. How shocked she must have been at my apallingly bad manners. I could not hold back the deep sigh, as I thought of all her goodness to me ... and the reason behind it all; a sigh that seemed to ricochet round the coach, causing everyone to look at me.

I remembered that on that occasion I had slept much of the way and now decided that it was indeed the best manner to pass away the tedious miles, so gripping my reticule tightly between my hands, I lay back and closed my eyes. I must have been exceptionally tired, for I did not wake until the noise and bustle of a coaching inn aroused me, and I became aware that we had arrived in Manchester.

Now I began to feel excited. Here I was on the threshold of discovery. I followed the maid up to my room, and was delighted to find it airy and comfortable-looking. Would I dine in my own room, or in the public dining-room? Oh yes, I was assured, ladies unaccompanied did dine in the public room.

I washed and changed into the other gown I had brought. How I missed having a maid to fasten my back tapes and hooks. I brushed and burnished my curls, and then with a dab of Spanish wool, went downstairs.

The chamber-maid in passing on my order for dinner had thoughtfully added that I was travelling alone, so that a table in a secluded corner had been reserved for me. As I entered, I could feel all eyes were upon me, male and female, and when, having seated myself, I looked around, I saw admiration in the men's eyes; disdain in the women's. The food was good, and I enjoyed every morsel of it, not having had a real meal for two days . . . since George's dinner-party.

Now I must begin to make my plans, and accordingly asked the serving-maid about hiring a coach. Yes, one could be hired from this inn; all I had to do was to state the time it was required . . . and pay in advance. Curton, I was told, was about fifteen miles outside Manchester.

Excitement and the nagging fear of

what I might find kept me awake that night. Might it not be better to let the past remain buried? What manner of life lay ahead of me? When I thought of what might have been, the tears came until I fell into a fitful doze.

★ ★ ★

I came down to the dining-room, attempting to look as nonchalant as though I was a most widely-travelled young lady, but beyond a cup of tea, I was unable to take of the ample breakfast offered.

My carriage had been ordered for ten o'clock, but I was out in the yard long before, so anxious was I to be on my way.

As we left the centre of the town, the streets and buildings became less impressive, gradually merging into ugly, sordid slums, with villainous looking men, slatternly woman and ragged children squatting about on the verges.

Then came new buildings with tall chimneys . . . obviously the new factories that were springing up all over the north. They were indeed an eyesore, but if they brought work for those idle men, which meant food for hungry women and children, why then they must be tolerated.

As we began to travel alongside a canal, I knew we were not far from my destination. From the carriage window, I looked at the dirty, muddy water, with its customary floating debris, and shuddered. The canal, at least, had not changed.

The coachman put me down in the centre of Curton. It was only a small town, with one main street and several others running off both right and left, but where to start my search, I was at a complete loss. I arranged with my driver to return within two hours, which I argued with myself was surely long enough to locate Mr. Barton and ask a few simple, but oh so vitally important questions.

I blithely entered the biggest and most prosperous looking shop, a general dealer's, asking could I be directed to the home of Mr. Barton. The woman regarded me with vague curiosity. I felt the heat rush to my face, at first shaking her head, she then said dryly, 'There's lots of Bartons round here . . . but none your sort . . . '

I could tell by the leer on her face that she thought I was in pursuit of some man, so I tried to be explicit.

'He is an elderly man . . . a working man . . . and I know he lives somewhere around here . . . '

'Try the ale-house, dearie. That's where most of the men spend their time.'

I thanked her, knowing full well I could not, indeed I dare not enter an ale-house. Where next? Coming along towards me, was a man, who, by his clothing, was obviously a clergyman. Dare I accost him? Surely he would know all the names of his parishioners, but when I reached him, my courage fled. A lady never speaks first . . . most definitely not to a stranger.

Something familiar about my surroundings brought me to a halt. Then the awful reality dawned upon me, I was standing outside the workhouse main entrance. The bricks around the door were crumbling and the door frame looked as though it was going to collapse at any time. I glanced up at the windows, built too high for the inmates to look out, and shuddered as I noted the filth on them; filth of many a year's collection. I turned and hurried away as quickly as possible.

I must find Ned Barton for he was the only man who could help me despite his now being married to the fearsome Mrs. Mathews. At the thought of meeting her again, I quailed, but only for a moment, plucking up my receding courage with the thought of having come so far, I must go on. Never for a moment did I consider danger.

As I turned the corner, Curton

church loomed before me; the church, where every Sunday, we pauper children were taken to thank God for all the benefits bestowed on us.

I remembered how we were herded into the back pews; how I used to watch and envy the little girls in their white frocks walk down the aisle into the front pews, holding on to their Mama's hand, oh, so tightly. I remembered how the parson always spared some time from his sermon to denounce those wicked children who during the week . . . and then he would read out misdemeanours any of us had perpetrated, together with the awful punishments we might expect unless we mended our evil ways.

We had to wait until the rest of the congregation had left; to suffer their stares; to see those little girls again, oh so demure, till they reached us, and then when Mama wasn't looking, sticking their tongues out at us.

Of course we retaliated; and of course, Mama always saw and reported us to Mrs. Mathews, which meant a whipping and no dinner.

Something impelled me to push open the door and enter. It was just as I remembered. A piece of unswept rush matting the length of the aisle; one small stained glass window in the chancel; the other windows so small that they let in but little light. For some strange, unaccountable reason, I found myself seated in that back pew. As before, there were no hassocks; pauper children still had to kneel on the dusty, bare floor. I knelt down. I prayed. I prayed for guidance. I prayed that neither George nor Julian should suffer too great a disappointment.

As I left the church, I almost collided with the clergyman I had previously encountered. Now I had no inhibition about speaking to him. He was not the same reverend gentleman who I had dreaded in my childhood; he looked human.

We both apologised at the same moment and it was he who opened the conversation.

'You have been looking over my church?'

I smilingly acquiesced, having no intention of telling him of my connection, going on to say, 'Actually, I am in Curton looking for a certain Mr. Barton.'

'Ah . . . I have several parishioners of that name. Have you any idea of his address?'

'Regretfully, no . . . '

'His occupation . . . his age?'

'He is elderly, or at least middleaged.' Then I remembered. 'He was a widower . . . but he remarried. A certain Mrs. Mathews.'

'Ah yes . . . I remember re-marrying a Ned Barton. Not so long ago . . . '

'If you could give me his address, sir . . . '

'He is some relative of yours?'

'Of a kind . . . '

He then directed me as to the road I should take. Ned Barton lived some distance out of Curton and as I left the ugly little town behind, I was delighted to find myself walking between the hedge-rows, with the odd row of cottages here and there. It was good that I was fond of walking, for my destination proved further than I had been led to believe, but at last I was walking up the narrow path of a well-kept, diminutive garden of an equally well-kept cottage.

I knocked on the door, while within me, my heart was beating rapidly, so that when a young woman opened it, I found my speech would come but spasmodically. Somehow I managed to blurt out my enquiry, only to be answered by a shake of the head.

'But . . . but Mr. Barton did live here, did he not?'

'I believe so, ma'am, but we have only just come. My Fred and I can't believe our good fortune in getting this place so soon after our wedding. We thought we should have to live with his mother until . . . '

I wasn't really listening; only conscious of bitter disappointment. No, she didn't know where the Bartons had gone; in fact she knew nothing about them whatever.

I thanked her and dismally retraced my steps down the little path. As I was re-fastening the sneck, a blowsy woman hanging over the next garden gate, arms akimbo, asked laconically, 'Looking for Ned Barton?'

'Why, yes, ma'am. Could you tell me as to where he has moved?'

'Not I. He went in too big a hurry to tell anyone. Did a moonlight-flit.'

I put my hand into my reticule. ' . . . and you have no idea where he went?'

'No . . . not really' The words came slowly. 'But Ned often talked about getting himself a job in one of the new factories, just outside Manchester . . . '

' . . . and you think I might find him at one or the other?'

'Where else?'

I gave her a guinea piece knowing that she could tell me no more. The obvious delight with which she grabbed it, only added to my despondency.

Now the long walk back to Curton faced me, but I was too engrossed with my chaotic thoughts to mind. How could I expect to find a man I didn't know? Of course, by going to the workhouse, I could find the new Mrs. Barton, but that would be putting myself in the power of the horrible creature. Besides, she didn't know anything about my birth, unless Ned Barton had told her. Should I go back to Yorkshire this very day? I felt so dispirited that I began to consider George's suggestion. Instead of all my fine, brave plans of standing on my own feet . . . of going on the stage . . . would I not be wiser to accept a post in the Perriman household as a companion to the children? No. I could never live under the same roof as George.

Back at the inn, I threw myself on the bed, completely exhausted and was soon asleep. I awoke feeling hungry. Little wonder, when I recalled that

I had not eaten since last night. It was dark, but groping my way to the fireplace, I pulled the bell for candles and hot water.

By the time I was ready to go downstairs, I felt a new person. I was staying in Manchester until I had found Ned Barton.

The dining-room was full, a couple of men of the city type occupying my secluded corner, so that I had to take a vacant seat at a table together with a family party. The meal was spoiled for me by the continuous wrangling between husband and wife; and the frequent carping at the children, which truth to tell, was well warranted, for their table-manners were deplorable; so bad, that I was glad to get away as quickly as possible. I would go to bed early, for I was planning a busy day for the morrow.

At the foot of the staircase I found my way barred by the two city men, laughingly eyeing me as I stood, not knowing what to say or do.

'The pretty lady is a stranger to Manchester is she not? We would like to take you round to see the sights . . . '

'Will you please let me pass?'

'My, oh my! The little lady doesn't think we're elegant enough.' The speaker jangled some coins in his pocket. 'Anywhere you want to go . . . you just say . . . '

'I want to go to my room . . . '

'Good. Then we'll come with you . . . '

The leering laugh was too much for me, as I realised with horror that they intended following me. Almost without thinking, I swung my arm high, and struck one of them full in the face with my reticule, which contained along with several other hard objects, my heavy glass smelling-bottle. His cry of rage, followed by a string of curses intermixed with the ribald laughter of his friend followed me up the stairs.

Once in the safety of my room, I shot home the bolt. Oh, the indignity of it all. That men should think I looked the type of female who was willing to be picked up. Of course, the fact that I was alone, lent colour to that situation; a situation that I must learn to live with.

* * *

I went down to breakfast early, hoping to get my corner table and to avoid those men. I would ask the serving maid that I might breakfast alone. To my chagrin, one man was already seated there, his back towards me. I looked around to choose another table, when something compelled me to look again in the man's direction. There was something familiar about the shape of the back of his head, and his broad shoulders. At the same moment, as though aware he was being scrutinised, he turned and our eyes met. It was George Perriman.

He rose to his feet, awaiting me, and as though mesmerised, I walked towards him, my heart clamouring that he might take me in his arms.

'George! What are you doing here? How did you know where . . . ?'

He took my hand and kissed it, at the same time putting me in the chair opposite. 'One question at a time, my darling. What am I doing here? Looking for you of course. How did I know where to look? Simple. Mr. Long told me you had taken the Manchester coach. It was easy to deduce you would stay at the coaching inn, knowing nothing of other Manchester hotels.'

'But why have you followed me?' I felt as petulant as a child who has been caught after running away.

He ignored my question, merely stating nonchalantly, 'Your Mr. Masters has arrived . . . '

He must have heard the sharp intake of my breath for he continued, 'No need for your alarm, dear Sophy. Indeed, everything is quite amicable between us . . . '

'You gave him my letter . . . ?'

'I did. He was quite devastated poor

fellow. You are a cruel little monster, Sophy. Nevertheless, he recovered sufficiently to join me and Mr. Stevens in a business consultation.' Was George laughing at me. He seemed to be in mighty fine spirits.

'It would appear my father's estate was almost bankrupt. Then he met up with Mr. Masters . . . both keen on reform. The outcome was, that when Mr. Masters told of the factory he was building in Yorkshire, my father expressed a wish to become a partner, putting into the business his last few thousands . . . '

'I knew the late Lord Perriman was interested,' I murmured.

' . . . and now I am interested! I am Mr. Masters' new partner. I am a man of business, Sophy.'

He regarded me with amusement, seeing the bewilderment of my face. 'But now it is I, the cruel monster, for I have left until the last, the most glorious, wonderful piece of news. After our business meeting last night, there was Mr. Long, requesting to speak to me in private. Oh Sophy my darling, you'll never guess . . . ' He had leaned across the table and taken my hands in his. I felt that the rest of the breakfast room must be watching us.

He signalled to a serving girl and ordered tea and toast. 'You must eat something, Sophy . . . '

'What is this you have to tell me . . . ?'

'Not in this crowded room, beloved . . . '

I had a queer lurching feeling in my stomach that he had learned something about me . . .

'Eat some of that toast, then we'll get out of here and go somewhere where we can really talk . . . '

I pushed away my plate. I could not eat, but the hot tea was reviving to my tormented mind.

Bidding him wait, I ran upstairs to get my cloak and when I rejoined him, it was to find he had hired a carriage, his own horses and coachman needing rest after travelling all last night.

'Where are we going?' I asked dispiritedly.

'Anywhere, out in the country where we can talk.'

'It's no use, George . . . '

We had reached the stable-yard and George was handing me into the coach and having given orders to the driver, seated himself beside me.

'George . . . please tell me what it was that Mr. Long . . . '

For answer, he enfolded me in his arms, holding me in a tight embrace as he kissed me hard and long. Then, gently, he released me, 'Just this, my darling, that you are free to marry me . . . that you are not my sister . . . '

'But how did Mr. Long . . . ?'

He silenced me with another kiss. 'On the night that Martha died, he had visited her earlier in the evening. It was a miracle he said, her voice coming back . . . sufficiently to tell the truth about . . . about Mama's baby . . . it had died at birth . . . so you see, Sophy, you cannot refuse me any longer, especially now that you have admitted you do not love Mr. Masters.'

'Don't torment me George. How can I marry you? Whoever I am, I am not a fit person to marry you. I am a nobody. Probably born in a ditch . . . the bastard of some low-living vagabond woman . . . !'

'Stop it, Sophy! Stop it! Even if what you suggest was proved true, I should still want to marry you. I am the judge of your worth.'

Never had I loved him more than in this moment of revelation. Gone was the shy, hesitant boy, who had relied on me to make the decisions in our childish affairs. Here was a man who knew his own mind.

'But your family,' I essayed weakly . . . ' . . . your sisters . . . That is why I didn't tell . . . '

He looked at me keenly as I came to a sudden stop. 'Didn't tell? Didn't tell what?'

'Nothing . . . I . . . I . . . '

'Sophy you cannot lie to me. Did you already know something? Something Martha told you?'

I could find no words to reply.

'Why did you not tell me?'

'Why did not Mr. Long tell you immediately?' I countered.

'I too asked that question. Apparently, he was communing with his conscience as to the advisability . . . fearing of hurting both you and me still more. It was something you told him during your drive to catch the mail coach that decided him. And now, I'm still waiting to hear, why you held out on me?'

I shook my head.

'Then I'll tell you. You were afraid my sisters would say you had invented the story. Am I not right? And because of that, you would have ruined both our lives. Oh Sophy, thank God for Martha and Mr. Long!'

Suddenly, I knew I was defeated but my defeat was my glory. I wanted George just as he wanted me. Forgetting all lady-like decorum. I flung my arms around his neck, 'Hold me tight, George. Never let me go again.'

How long I stayed there in the shelter of his arms, I do not know. I felt so at rest, but at last George was murmuring, 'We had better be getting back to the inn, in order that we might begin our return journey . . .'

'But I am staying here, George . . . at least until . . .'

'Until what, Sophy?'

'Until I have accomplished what I came to do . . . to establish my parentage . . .'

'Then as yet, I take it you have made no progress . . . ?'

I told him of my futile efforts, but ending firmly, 'But I am going to find that man if I have to visit every factory in Manchester . . .'

'And then what?'

'I don't know . . . I just don't know . . .'

'But I do, my darling. You're

marrying me at the first possible moment.'

'No matter what sordid facts we unearth?'

'No matter.' He opened the window and called to the coachman to turn round and take us to the nearest factory.

'Your idea of visiting every factory seems the only practical way . . . but I will do the talking. 'Tis hardly a task for a young lady.'

We spent the whole day driving from one factory to another, waiting to see factory owners, managers, foremen, and it wasn't until we visited the fifth that we ran Ned Barton to earth. By this time we were famished and exhausted, but armed with Mr. Barton's address, we returned to the inn, jubilant and excited. Yet, hungry as we were, we could not face sitting down to dinner, contenting ourselves with a glass of wine and a biscuit.

Then we were on our way to Ned Barton's lodging. It turned out to be a mean room in a tumble-down house in one of Manchester's poorest quarters. At first, he was disinclined to ask us in, but George's gentle, persuasive manner soon assured him that he had nothing to fear.

The room was ill-lit, there being only one small oil-lamp but as we entered from the dark landing, Ned Barton stared at me, a wild look in his eyes, exclaiming, 'It's her . . . It's her . . . '

How thankful I was to notice that Mrs. Barton, formerly Mrs. Mathews was not at home. I had been dreading meeting her again.

George was in command of the situation without any fluster or flurry, asking, 'Could we not all sit down and discuss our business. Now Mr. Barton, for whom did you mistake this lady?'

'It's her right enough . . . just as she came to us that day. Those golden-red curls . . . how could anyone forget them? . . . Your're her bairn, aren't you?'

I found my voice. 'I don't know. That's why I'm here . . . Please, Mr. Barton . . . who was she, who came to you?'

'She was an actress woman . . . '

I almost jumped from my chair. An actress? 'What was her name.'

'Her name? A lovely name. As sweet as herself. Felicity. Felicity Kent. Poor dear girl. She was with child, playing in Manchester until it should be born, then intending to go back to London.'

I was saying the name softly under my breath. 'Felicity. Felicity Kent.'

' . . . Her lover . . . some fine gentleman had been generous. She was not without money and did not wish to embarrass him in anyway . . . '

'And after the child was born, did she go back to London?'

He shook his head. 'No, Miss, no. She died.'

A black, dreadful silence enveloped the room. It was George who asked the question. ' . . . And what happened to the child?'

Ned Barton made a gesture of helplessness. 'Everything went wrong that night. My wife, apart from being a midwife, also fostered bairns . . . bairns from good families . . . you understand, sir . . . outside the blanket. Well, that night we were expecting such a one . . . to be looked after until the mother could make other arrangements to look after it herself. There was a goodly sum of money handed over and the promise of more to come. Then after the old nurse had gone . . . and where she came from, we never knew . . . we found the bairn was dead . . . '

' . . . and so you had a dead woman and a dead baby in the house?' George's voice was low and compassionate.

'Yes, sir . . . and could you have done anything different from what we did? We buried the poor young woman with the unknown baby in her arms. She had enough money for a decent funeral. We did not rob her, sir.'

'I'm sure you did not. But her child . . . '

'Little red-head? Yelling her lungs out, she was, but she grew into a regular little charmer, sir, and the wife used to dress her up . . . a right little beauty she was. About every six months, money would arrive by post . . . a little new dress . . . a cape and hood, all edged with fur . . . and toys . . . but we didn't have any address to write and say the child was dead.'

'So you used it for the upbringing of the other one?'

'Why, yes sir. What else could we do?'

'Nothing. I am happy to think it was so used . . . '

'Then both my wife and I went down with the pox and within a few days she was dead. The authorities came and took the bairn and when I was well enough, I started up as a tally-man to get away from the place . . . to forget . . . '

'But the money still came?'

'Yes, I felt bad about keeping it but why should I give it to the Institution?

After all, the money wasn't sent for that bairn, and, in any case, she wouldn't have benefited if I had handed it over. If I could have found a decent woman to marry, I would have had the child back . . . but it didn't happen that way.'

'No, but the day did come, did it not when you had a visitor, asking for the child who died . . . and you told the story of your wife's death and the little girl's transfer into the Institution . . . knowing full well it was a lie . . . '

It was remarkable how George was piecing the story together.

'Aye . . . but the old woman was in deep a pother as I was. She couldn't let on about me without giving herself away. She knew the baby was dead when she handed it over but it was obvious she hadn't told anyone. She made it clear that I should keep the money and I would hear no more about it. Later on, I was told the bairn had been taken to Yorkshire to work in some great lady's kitchen. I could never understand it. Working it out, it seemed to me, as though that serving woman, never having told her mistress the babe was dead was at a loss which way to turn when the lady wished to reclaim her child. Was another hapless little brat foisted in her place?' He looked at me keenly, continuing to mutter, 'Funny business. Funny business.' I could not repress the excited curiosity in my voice. 'Now that I am sure my mother stayed with you, could you tell me more about her?'

'What can I tell you, miss, beyond she was such a happy creature, always singing and playing on her guitar; planning for the future. She was going to leave you with us until she found employment in London and was in a position to have you with her.'

'And my father? Did she never speak of him?'

'Very rarely . . . but she left something that I must give you.'

He went over to a box in the corner of the room, untying the cords and from its depths taking out a small parcel wrapped in faded news-sheet. My hands trembled with excitement as I tore the paper away, and then I found myself gazing at a minature, set in pearls, for which I might have been the sitter. I knew it was my mother.'

' . . . and on the other side,' suggested Ned Barton.

I turned it over. It was the minature of a man; a young man of haughty, aristocratic demeanour, wearing a modish wig. Presumably, my father.

'I'm glad to be rid of it, miss. I never dare let Mrs. Mathews see it . . . '

'You must allow me to reward you for your honesty . . . ' George was taking several golden coins from his guinea-case. 'Why did you never sell it?'

'Too risky, sir. Too many questions would have been asked . . . '

We took our leave, George assuring Mr. Barton that he would hear no more of the matter. As we drove away, we were both immersed in our own thoughts. We had almost reached the inn before George spoke. 'Well, Sophy, are you now satisfied with what you have learned?'

For a moment, I didn't answer. Then, 'The Felicity Kent Orphanage' ... 'The Felicity Kent Children's Home' ... or better still 'The Kent-Perriman Home,' or should it be the 'Perriman-Kent Home'? Which do you think, sir?'

'Perhaps, dear heart, you would enlighten me, as to what ... '

'I am going to found a children's home. Aunt Lucy left me some money. I shall use it ... a home for unwanted children ... where they will be wanted ... and cared for ... '

'You are entitled to do as you wish with your own money ... '

'There is also a substantial dowry ... '

'So Mr. Stevens informed me.' There was a dry humour in his voice. 'I wonder, whether the lady who is founding this home, would allow me to be a subscriber . . . an active subscriber. I have a good head for figures and finance . . . '

'Oh George! Do you really mean you will help me?'

'Isn't that what a loving husband should do? But apart from this project, how do you feel, now that you have learned . . . '

'Truth to tell, sir, I am still much confused, but at least, I do know I am of decent birth even though I am a bastard. My mother had no intention of deserting me. I don't suppose she ever thought she might die . . . ' My voice trailed away, almost lost in the threatened sobs . . . 'and poor Aunt Lucy. How she must have suffered both before and after her baby was born. No wonder Martha stooped to deceit to bring her comfort. All those waiting years of grief . . . Martha knowing the truth . . . yet never telling. Was it very wrong?'

'Who are we to judge? But I thank

God and my mother that you were rescued from that dreadful place . . . '

'As long as I live, I shall never cease to be grateful to Aunt Lucy . . . and Martha . . . '

' . . . remembering, dear heart, that at the same time you served a purpose, giving comfort and joy to my mother who firmly believed that you were her child . . . '

' . . . and all that time her baby was sleeping in my mother's arms. I like to think of that, George.'

'Yes. Strange to think of it . . . your mother . . . my mother and now . . . It's all over, Sophy. We must not dwell on it. You and I are together for all time.'

'The Perrimans will want to know of my parentage . . . '

'I can deal with them . . . and show them that minature. That will quickly silence them . . . '

His arms were around me, murmuring, 'and now, my very dearest love, how soon can we be married?'

I lifted my face to his. 'As soon as ever it can be arranged.' Then I was lost in wonder at the perfection of our love, as we clung to each other, exchanging kiss for kiss.

As we pulled up outside the inn, I asked 'Do you think your coachman and your horses will be sufficiently rested?'

'I should think so, my love. Why do you ask?'

'Then we will drive back to Yorkshire this very night . . .'

'But Sophy, after such a day, you must be worn out . . .'

'I can sleep in your arms, can I not?'

'But Sophy, my darling . . .'

'You are thinking of the proprieties, George? Remember, I am the daughter of an actress and I've probably inherited some of the brazen ways all actresses are supposed to have . . .'

'Sophy! You are a torment! A dear, adorable torment, but you shall have your way. To hold you in my arms, throughout the night, is more than I can resist.'

'But you will make an honest woman of me?' I teased.

Holding me firmly by the arms and looking straight into my eyes, he answered in mock severity, 'Mr. Long is waiting to perform the ceremony . . . Julian Masters is waiting to give you away. Is there anything else you require?'

'Yes. Tell me once again you love me.'

Despite the coachman, waiting to open the door, George complied in a manner that needed no words.

THE END

NEATH PORT TALBOT LIBRARY
AND INFORMATION SERVICES

1		25		49	71/2	73	
2		26		50	7/17	74	
3		27		51		75	
4	7/01	28		52		76	
5		29		53		77	
6	3/18	30		54		78	
7		31		55		79	
8		32		56		80	
9		33		57		81	
10		34		58	11/14	82	5/05
11		35		59		83	
12		36	9/03	60		84	
13	11/18	37	2/19	61		85	
14	2/18	38		62		86	
15	5/16	39		63		87	
16	9/16	40		64		88	
17		41		65		89	
18		42		66		90	
19	9/00	43		67		91	4/15
20		44		68		92	
21		45	8/9	69		COMMUNITY SERVICES	
22		46	4/04	70			
23	2/14	47		71		NPT/111	
24	6/05	48		72	7/18		